SEOPY

SEOPYEONJE

THE SOUTHERNERS' SONGS

YI CHUNG-JUN

Translated by Ok Young Kim Chang

With a foreword by Michael J. Pettid

London and Chicago

PETER OWEN PUBLISHERS
20 Holland Park Avenue, London W11 3QU

Peter Owen books are distributed in the USA and Canada by
Independent Publishers Group/Trafalgar Square
814 North Franklin Street, Chicago, IL 60610, USA

English translation first published in Great Britain 2011
by Peter Owen Publishers

Stories 'Seopyeonje' (1976), 'The Light of Songs' (1976), 'Immortal Crane
Village' (1979), 'Bird and Tree' (1980), 'The Rebirth of Words' (1981)
first collected and published as *Seopyeonje* in 1993

Translated from the Korean *Seopyeonje*
© Estate of Yi Chung-jun (Nam Kyung-ja) 1993

Translation © Ok Young Kim Chang 2011
Foreword © Michael J. Pettid 2011
Cover photograph © Tae-Heung Films Co. Ltd 1993

ISBN 978-0-7206-1359-9

A catalogue record for this book is available from the British Library.

Printed and bound by CPI Group (UK) Ltd, Croydon, CR0 4YY

**This book is published with the support of the
Korea Literature Translation Institute.**

Typeset by Octavo-Smith Ltd in Constantia 10.5/14

FOREWORD

KOREA HAS AN old and deep literary tradition, with written works perhaps dating back some 1,800 years or more. As with any ancient literature, the earliest works are not easily dated or even identified with a particular writer. While the passage of time has thus made it difficult to clarify an absolute beginning, we know that writing and works of literature became an important focus of the upper levels of society from a very early point in Korean history – in particular, writing systems were adopted from Chinese states no later than the late Three Kingdoms period (*c*. the fifth century CE) and most likely much earlier. The transmission of ideological systems such as Buddhism and Confucianism from China in the fourth century CE certainly hastened this process. In fact, the quest for knowledge became an important component in expanding literary activities in Korea. By the late eighth century a government-service examination based on knowledge of Confucianism was implemented in the Silla Kingdom (57BCE–935CE), and, with few pauses, such examinations remained the means for selecting government officials until the late nineteenth century. This system that stressed education fostered the growth of literature and helped place it at the pinnacle of pre-modern Korean societies.

An interesting aspect of Korean literature is that while Koreans certainly speak a language that is distinct from their Chinese neighbours, for centuries Koreans used Chinese as their written language. Such a situation was certainly not unique in Asia, as the peoples of Japan and Vietnam followed a similar pattern. Even after the Korean script, known as hangeul, was created in the early fifteenth century, literary forms written in Chinese characters were given a higher status than those written in the vernacular script. Thus we have a situation where the great bulk of pre-modern written literature was written in a language other than that spoken by the Korean people. This naturally created a hierarchy not only of literary forms – where those written in Chinese characters were given more value – but created a division of readership between those who could read the Chinese texts and those who could not.

Adding to the preference given to texts written in Chinese was the hegemonic position given to Confucianism and the Confucian canon in Korea. Confucianism was crucial to the administration of Korean states – especially from the fifteenth century onwards – and the focus on examination systems based on this ideology had great effect on literature, if for no other reason than that the educated elite had spent their lives studying Confucian texts. Consequently, pre-modern literature in Korea was heavily influenced by Confucian thought and orthodoxy, often to the exclusion of forms that did not follow the strict accords of Confucian morality. This backdrop led to poetic forms –especially those in Chinese characters – being given much higher status than fictional forms of prose.

Elites naturally favoured forms that reflected the world in which they lived. They favoured poetic styles that were similar to those of China, as were the various forms of prose they used. On the other hand, those not educated in Chinese had no choice but to use different means to share literature. Before the creation of hangeul these were exclusively oral forms. The art of performing literature as a means of transmission became finely tuned as a result, and many folk songs, poem-songs and shaman's songs were passed from generation to generation for centuries before being written down.

It is certainly possible to view these all as these various forms of literature as being distinct, and, indeed, they can stand alone and be examined or appreciated for their various qualities and for their beauty. Yet the complexity and the depth of Korean literature is best appreciated when we look at the amalgamation of these various styles, forms and genres in the singular style of pansori, a type of one-person dramatic story-singing.

How can we best locate pansori in pre-modern Korean literature? To begin, we need to understand how literature was viewed in pre-modern Korea, particularly in the Joseon dynasty (1392–1910). For the upper-class elites of Joseon, literature was not so much an entertainment as a moral exercise in which a man could, through the composition of poetry, demonstrate his understanding of Confucian morality and self-reflection. The creation of literature was seen as an exercise that helped one reach a higher plateau of ethical purity. Consider this brief poem by Yun Seon-do (1587–1671) who is counted among the best poets of the Joseon era. Entitled 'Ou-ga' ('The Song of the Five Friends'), the first verse reads:

How many friends have I? There are water, stone,
    pine and bamboo.
As the moon rises over the eastern mountain,
    I am all the more delighted.
Ah, with these five friends, what need do I have of more?

The sentiments of the poem are both simple and profound and reflect the quest by elites in this period to take in the beauty of nature while reflecting on improving oneself. Isolation from the mundane matters of the world was the norm in these poems as was viewing nature as a type of perfected morality. But this is a decidedly rarefied poem and world view, the work of a writer far removed from everyday matters such as farming and the daily hardships of life. A poem such as this one could only have been created by someone who had transcended such mundane matters as earning a living or toiling in fields.

However, Joseon, like perhaps all societies, had different social codes depending upon time and place. Thus the Confucianist who sought to improve himself in one poem might have also found time to share poems and wine with others. Furthermore, prose works offered a place to tell stories and had a definite entertainment element lacking in many poems. So, even among those of the highest class, literature was multifaceted and did not adhere only to the strict ideals of Confucianism.

Making the picture even more unclear was the wave of literature that followed the creation of the Korean script hangeul, in the early fifteenth century. While this writing system was primarily created as a means to educate the masses in Confucian ideology, it soon took on a life of its own, as the easily mastered phonetic writing system was ideal for those of lower status – commoners, and the low-born, along with women who were not often trained in Chinese characters – to write their own stories. The common classes and women had always had oral literature, but now they had a means to write down their stories, songs and poems. This was nothing short of a revolution in Korean literature, and an explosion of literary creations ensued from the sixteenth century onwards.

While poetry continued to be upheld as the highest form of literature by those of the upper ranks of society, in the second half of Joseon we see the blossoming of other forms. New and longer poetic styles came into vogue that allowed the greater development of themes and the experiences of the writers. These forms also matched with performed literature such as the folk songs that had long been popular among the common folk as work songs and as a means to pass on colourful tales. The expansion of the group creating literature to include those from nearly all social strata permitted an even greater range of voices, life experiences and emotions to be expressed in literary form. It was no longer just the domain of the elite but had now shifted to the masses.

Works of fiction also blossomed in the time after the creation of hangeul. Fiction was in general held in disdain by the ruling classes, even to the point of periodically attempting to restrict the creation of such works. None the less, forms such as the novel proved to be highly popular among many groups of people and perhaps most among women. Novels provided an expanded space to tell stories and fully develop characters and their lives. Various genres, including heroic novels, romances and allegorical works became prominent from the seventeenth century onwards and enjoyed large readerships. The fictional spaces served many functions in society such as creating alternative realities where those of lower social groups could experience better lives for themselves. The novel as a tool for social criticism is clearly seen in the works of this time, and no doubt was a key factor in its popularity.

From this milieu arose pansori. While storytelling and travelling entertainers had long been a feature of Korean culture, the advent of this genre is relatively recent when one considers it in the context of Korean literature. The first records of pansori are in the seventeenth century, but the oral tradition from which it arose dates to the earliest Korean societies. The penchant of Koreans for song and dance is recorded in some of the earliest historical records about the people of the Korean peninsula, and such a love continues to the present day. Pansori is the maturation of such a cultural trait, and these songs harvest content from both long-standing folk traditions, including masked-dance dramas, shaman songs and folk tales, together with written literary forms such as the novel to create compelling narratives that are able to grasp the attention of audiences and tap into a wealth of deep-seated emotions. While the basic narratives are well known to nearly all Koreans, it is the performance aspect of the songs that keeps audiences returning. The successful pansori singer is one who can convey the emotions and energy of a song and impart this to his or her audience. Much like the acclaimed opera singers of Western tradition, the singers of pansori became famous through their ability to draw audiences with their storytelling talents.

Initially it was the strong bond with everyday life that made pansori so popular among the lower-born groups that first followed these songs. The elements of the songs were borrowed liberally from folk tales and legends, which were the literary creations of the masses. Hence audiences saw their own lives reflected in the songs and felt strong bonds with the hardships and triumphs of the protagonists. Moreover, like many oral genres, the songs were at times highly critical of the upper levels of society, so this social criticism was also reflective of the minds of the people who frequented these performances. The singers of the songs were also of the people. Entertainers were considered a low-born class in Joseon, so the hardships of which they sung reflected their own lives as well as that of their audience.

The performers of pansori were part of a group of entertainers known as *gwangdae*. In general, singing or entertainment was their only livelihood, and they learned their craft from their families, as this was mostly a hereditary occupation. The successful singer was one who could quickly read his or her audience and change the performance to match a particular crowd. We could expect that in a marketplace performance mostly watched by commoners the critique of the ruling class would have been more prominent than in a performance held at the home of a wealthy person. Such interaction determined a successful singer.

Simplicity was the rule for pansori. To perform, a singer needed just the accompaniment of a drummer. The stage could be anywhere, and no props were required. In performance, pansori singers use a mixture of spoken and sung passages together with asides to the drummer and the audience. The drummer, in addition to beating out rhythm on a barrel-drum, shouts encouragement to the singer during the performance. Singers also use gesture and movement to increase the entertainment value of their story. This mixture of spoken and sung passages, together with dramatic gestures and audience interaction, creates a performance with a varied pace and allows the singer respite from the difficulties of singing for prolonged periods of time.

The number of pansori performed was never great: it seems that there were twelve songs performed by the nineteenth century, but this number diminished to just five by the beginning of the twentieth century. Within the narrative of the present volume four are mentioned: *The Song of Sim Cheong, The Song of Chunhyang, The Song of the Water Palace* and *The Song of Hongbo and Nolbu*. A short description of these songs might give a better understanding of the contents and the social functions that led these to be popular.

The Song of Chunhyang remains a favourite narrative for Koreans even today. The song has been made into films numerous times and still draws good audiences when shown on television. The narrative is a rather typical story of good versus evil, a mismatched love affair and perseverance in the face of adversity. The main characters of this narrative are Chunhyang, the daughter of a female entertainer (a low-born character), and Yi Mong-ryong, the son of the Magistrate of Namwon (a member of the elite). The two meet, fall in love and are separated when Yi's family returns to the capital. A new magistrate is appointed to the city of Namwon who desires the beautiful Chunhyang, but she spurns his advances. Consequently, she is imprisoned, flogged and approaches death in her steadfast refusal of the magistrate's sexual advances. In the end she is rescued by Mong-ryong, who, after passing the government-service examination, is appointed as a secret royal inspector and returns to Namwon where he arrests the evil magistrate. Chunhyang is then reunited with her love, and they live happily together to a ripe old age.

What sort of message did this song hold for audiences in Joseon Korea? First, we can see the desire for freedom of choice in marriage. Joseon was not an egalitarian society, and marriage practices reflected this division of classes. The love affair described was certainly not permissible, especially from the standpoint of the elite. Second, we can note that there is a distinct discontent with the corruption and abuse of power by some government officials. The likes of Chunhyang would have had no means of opposing such a person. One could only hope that an honourable official would ride into town and save the day, although this would have been an unlikely event. Third, there is the issue of Chunhyang's fidelity, which would have been very important to the highest-status groups of Joseon, as Confucian dictates the importance of female chastity. Thus there is a blend of ideals in this song that would have touched the audience on many levels. The commoners in the audience would have shared the pain of Chunhyang in not realizing her love and also the inappropriate actions of the new magistrate. Upper-status people would have enjoyed the steadfast heart of Chunhyang in not yielding to the magistrate – and perhaps they, too, would have longed for freedom of choice in matters of the heart. Perhaps all listeners would have felt sympathy for the pain of the young woman suffering in her lover's absence.

The Song of Sim Cheong has a similar blend of upper- and lower-class values. The narrative tells of a blind and poor widower who struggles to raise his daughter Sim Cheong. She grows up to be a beautiful and devoted daughter, and when her father foolishly pledges three hundred sacks of rice to the Buddha to regain his eyesight she secretly sells herself for the same price to a group of sailors who wish to buy a young maiden to sacrifice at sea. After her sacrifice Sim Cheong is rescued by the Jade Emperor and eventually brought to the Emperor of China as a present. She ultimately becomes his empress and is reunited with her father who regains his eyesight at hearing the sound of her voice.

This song promotes a strong Confucian morality theme of devotion to one's parents. Sim Cheong embodies these ideals of filial piety, even going to the extent of sacrificing her life for that of her father. In Joseon, however, women did not enjoy the same rights as men and were greatly devalued by society. But audience members would have heard of a most capable woman, one who actually came back from the dead. This would have been greatly moving for the women in the audience, who no doubt suffered from the general repression of females at that time. The narrative also criticizes corrupt monks and features a common element in pre-modern Korean literature, the notion of supernatural intervention on behalf of the righteous. This, too, would have struck a chord with many in the audience who had their own hardships to endure and overcome. And, certainly, the happy ending of the story would have pleased the audience and aroused a desire in them for a similar outcome in their own lives, despite the overwhelming odds against attaining this.

The Song of the Water Palace stands alone among the existing pansori repertory in that it uses animals as its protagonists and personifies various human shortcomings in these creatures. The story begins with a description of the Dragon King of the sea, who becomes ill as a result of his libertine lifestyle. The royal doctor informs him that the only way he will survive is to eat the liver of a rabbit. The king calls together his court and asks of his many ministers which one of them will go to the terrestrial world and bring back a rabbit. Only one steps forward, a terrapin. The terrapin finds a rabbit and tricks him with promises of a high position, wealth and beautiful women to come to the underwater palace, but once there the rabbit understands that he has been lied to. Quick-witted, he concocts a story that he has left his liver onshore and that if he is allowed to return he will retrieve it and bring it to the Dragon King. However, once on land the rabbit flees, leaving behind the tricked terrapin.

This story has a long and far-flung history, having been transmitted to Korea from India via China. Originally, this was a Buddhist allegory that featured a monkey and crocodile, but these characters changed to meet local circumstances as the narrative moved eastwards. While this tale was originally a religious one, the pansori rendition is very much secular. This depiction of the dissolute lifestyle of the Dragon King and his self-serving ministers reveals the common people's perception of the royal court and ministers of Joseon. The rabbit, representing the governed classes, seeks to escape his difficult and dangerous life and is thus easily deceived by the promises of the terrapin. In the end, however, the rabbit outwits his captors and returns to his life on the land. Such a conclusion seems to indicate popular sentiments about the governing class.

The Song of Hongbo and Nolbu features two brothers, the elder Nolbu and younger Hongbo. After the death of their parents, Nolbu takes all their property and drives off his younger sibling. Hongbo, honest and kind-hearted, attempts to scratch out a living by some means, but his family struggles in terrible poverty. When he asks Nolbu for help, he is beaten and chased away. However, the kindly Hongbo stumbles upon an injured swallow. He mends its leg, and in the following year he is rewarded by the bird with a gourd seed that sprouts into a vine bearing riches of every sort. The Heavens have been kind to Hongbo, and he becomes a very wealthy man. Nolbu hears of this and intentionally injures a swallow in order to help it recover in the hope of becoming even wealthier. His reward is also a gourd seed, but from this spring forth evil creatures that ruin his home. Hongbo, hearing of this misfortune, shares half his wealth with his now repentant elder brother.

We can note common folk-tale storylines here such as the reward of good and punishment of evil by supernatural powers, repayment of good by animals, the harsh lives of farming families and the need for good relations among siblings. All of these would have resonated clearly with audiences, as they, too, would have undoubtedly been involved in situations in which they needed help. Certainly, the desire for a life of wealth was one that many in the audience would have found appealing, and this no doubt helped keep this song a popular one in the pansori repertoire. The hardships and suffering of

Hongbo were universal themes that common folk would have related to closely, and we can imagine their elation when the kind-hearted Hongbo is rewarded.

As the nineteenth century progressed, pansori became increasingly focused on the upper classes of Joseon, and singers could become quite wealthy as a result of the patronage of these aficionados. Thus critical elements and the view of commoners became less prominent and were replaced by allusions to classical literature and other interests of elite society. Furthermore, the singing styles of pansori separated into two main schools: the Eastern School (Dongpyeonje) and the Western School (Seopyeonje). The main difference between these two was emphasis on tradition versus ongoing efforts to refine and polish singing styles. The Western School sought to improve singing styles, and the singers of this school worked towards improving their techniques and the aesthetics of their songs. The result of this was growth and increased depth in singing styles and refinement of the beauty of pansori performances.

As with all things in Korea, pansori experienced great turmoil and change at the start of the twentieth century. The fall of the Joseon dynasty and the advent of the colonial period under Japan resulted in tremendous changes in nearly every aspect of society. New literary and musical styles entered Korea, and these were soon to have an adverse effect on the popularity of pansori. Many of the new singing styles reflected trends from the West, and these became widely popular. Against this backdrop pansori singers and their performances fell on hard times. This difficult situation continued throughout most of the twentieth century and is well reflected in the hard and itinerant life of the singer in this novel. From the apex of high culture in the late nineteenth century, by the second half of the twentieth century pansori had deteriorated to the status of a dusty remnant of a long-gone time that few Koreans cared to revisit.

By the mid-to-late 1980s some very important changes happened in South Korean society. Hand in hand with the democracy movement vigorously fought for and eventually won by college students and others was a quest for understanding 'authentic' Korean culture. The period after the Korean War (1950–53) was one of great economic growth and modernization in the South, but in the process many aspects of traditional culture were forgotten or pushed aside as backward or old-fashioned. Western classical music was popular among educated elites and jazz or rock music with others. Korean musical styles now mimicked those of the West, and traditional forms were rarely heard. However, in the pursuit of authentic culture, pansori, together with other traditional arts such as the masked-dance dramas, was rediscovered. While slow and never at the levels of the previous century, a resurgence occurred in pansori and helped usher in a new era of popularity and development of the art of storytelling.

The author of *Seopyeonje*, Yi Chung-jun, no doubt helped this revival. When the individual linked stories were collected and published as a novel in 1993 it had the effect of helping to awaken a desire among many to see this art form thrive once more and to experience a performance that was uniquely Korean. The popularity greatly increased with the release of the movie version of the novel, also entitled *Seopyeonje*, in 1993. Directed by Im Kwon Taek, the film won awards and was a box-office hit, and it brought pansori singing to a new and appreciative audience. This was an important milestone in the rebirth of the art form, and it has remained in the public eye ever since that time.

The present translation of Yi Chung-jun's novel captures much of the flavour and emotion of the Korean text. In the descriptions of remote villages in south-western Korea we can find glimpses of a time – forty or so years ago – that has long past and seems nearly remote as Joseon Korea. The author's style is purposefully disjointed and at times overly foreboding but none the less draws the reader into the psyche of his characters and their personal tribulations. The pilgrimage of the brother to find an 'answer' or some meaning in his life resembles a Buddhist quest for enlightenment in past times, especially in that the 'answer' he finds is not at all tangible. Brief and fleeting encounters, oddly matched pairings and surreal settings are all used to push the novel to a conclusion that is at the same time satisfying and perplexing. Much like the beauty of a pansori performance, the novel moves from the commonplace to the sublime and elicits emotions of both elation and sorrow, all the while keeping readers wondering what will happen next.

Professor Michael J. Pettid
Department of Asian and Asian American Studies
Binghamton University, New York

TRANSLATOR'S NOTE

PANSORI IS OFTEN described as one-person folk opera in which the singer – usually accompanied by a drummer – executes dialogue and narration as well as acting and singing. Seopyeonje, the Western School – as distinct from Dongpyeonje, the Eastern School – was developed in the region west of the Seomjingan River in Jeollanamdo Province, the southernmost province of the Korean Peninsula near the cities of Boseong, Naju and Yonggwang. The performance of a complete pansori takes anything from four to eight hours, and the texts are based on well-known legends that, traditionally, were transmitted orally. Originally pansori was performed by *gwangdae*, itinerant entertainers who were believed to be blood relations of the shaman and who usually occupied the lowest stratum in traditional Korean social structure. Pansori requires a heavy, hoarse vocal timbre, which is achieved through long training.

The Korean edition contains the following author's note: 'Some sections of "The Rebirth of Words", which concludes this cycle, are taken from another collection of linked stories entitled *An Introduction to the Sociology of Language.*'

CONTENTS

SEOPYEONJE

IN THE TAVERN the woman poured out her songs from early evening without stopping, oblivious to the pain in her throat, while the man accompanied her on his drum. His expression communicated an impression of strain in an effort to suppress a certain premonition stirred by the woman's songs. The sweat of labour had formed in clusters on the foreheads of both performers, the singer with her endless songs and the drummer mutely accompanying her.

The tavern stood on a quiet street corner on the outskirts of the town of Boseong, Jeolla-do Province, overlooking in the distance a group of hamlets on the left and a public burial ground on a steep hill on the right, where ancient graves were packed closely right to the edge of the street. The villagers called the secluded hilly passage that meandered through the cemetery the Song Pass, and everyone knew the name of the tavern, the Song Pass Tavern, a dust-coated thatched place that crouched like a clamshell at the entrance to the cemetery. No one suggested that it should be called anything else, since wailings and pallbearers' dirges filled the street, and the tavern stood guarding its entrance. Casual observers would have passed by without giving it any further thought. There was, however, something more to this passage and this tavern. Most villagers who understood what was what knew about it. Even strangers to the village, if they happened to stop at this tavern for a night of drinking, would soon learn of its significance. This was because of the songs the proprietress sang. She was unmarried and barely managed to keep the tavern going without the help of a man. So extraordinary was her skill in singing the songs of the southern region that anyone who listened to her was deeply moved.

The traveller must have known about the woman and her songs and not wandered into the tavern that night by chance. In fact, he had come with a clear expectation. He had spent the previous night in another town, and the innkeeper there had told him about the Song Pass. Without bothering to listen to the end of the story he left the inn and set off, following the prompting of a premonition.

When he arrived the traveller felt an atmosphere of something beyond the ordinary at the tavern: the woman's inexhaustible singing, which continued from early evening into the depths of the night. Behind the legend of the tavern were this woman's artistry – a woman barely thirty – and her proud, elegant rendition of the distinctive pansori songs from this southern region. As he listened his face betrayed an expression of discontent, as if his earlier ardent sense of anticipation had not been fully satisfied. The longer he listened, the more deeply he became lost in his thoughts. Moved to the depth of his soul by the sound of the songs, he did not notice the small table with wine that had been brought into the room. Finally, after the woman had sung a few scenes from *The Song of Chunhyang*,[1] he pushed aside the wine table and found himself asking for an instrument to accompany the woman.

'Fine, very fine indeed. Let us first wet our throats with this wine and continue,' he proposed.

After each scene had been sung he handed his wine cup to the woman, appreciating the need for liquid for the singer and the importance of urging her to continue. She executed a graceful rendition of *The Song of the Water Palace*.[2]

Eventually he could contain himself no longer. 'Tell me,' he asked at last, passing the cup once more to the woman to drink from, 'how long have you been singing – hiding yourself in a place like this?'

At first she looked puzzled, seeming not quite to have understood the meaning of the man's tentative enquiry, and remained silent, although her eyes were steadily fixed on him.

He continued, 'I came knowing that this place is called Song Pass and that your tavern is called the Song Pass Tavern. It must be because of the reputation of your songs. Isn't that so?'

Still she did not give him an answer, but this time her silence did not appear to suggest that she had misunderstood his question. Her mostly expressionless but gently probing eyes pursued him, trying to decipher his thoughts, then she slowly shook her head.

'Does this mean you are not the original cause of the legend of this place? Was there another before you?' the guest persisted impatiently. 'I take it then that there is another story that came before your songs?'

Only then did she move her head in acknowledgement. Her face began to cloud, and she spoke haltingly. 'You are right. The names of this pass and this tavern have nothing to do with my singing. I don't deserve them. There was one who could sing the real songs.'

'Who was that person? I ask you, who was that singer?' he demanded urgently, driven by foreboding.

'The one who is buried in the grave.'

'What grave?'

'At the top of this hill. We call it the "Song Grave". You have heard about the Song Pass and the Song Pass Tavern, yet you don't know the story of this man's grave. During his lifetime he knew nothing but songs, so the villagers filled his grave with his songs. The rest of the story came after that: the Song Pass and Song Pass Tavern.'

She could not fend off the traveller's barrage of questions and began her story of long-ago events in a voice tinged with sighs. The story went like this.

At the end of the Korean War, as peace returned to the country, the villagers began the process of recovery. It was during the autumn of 1956 or 1957. When the proprietress was still a child she had worked as a servant girl for a prosperous family in town in order to feed herself. To this grand household came two strange boarders, a father and daughter, two itinerant pansori singers. One day the head of the household, who was past sixty, had gone to town, where he met the singers by chance, and when he returned home he brought them with him. The old master installed the singers in the *sarang* quarters[3] and treated them as his guests. Their astounding artistry transported his spirit, and throughout the autumn he enjoyed listening to their songs.

The skills of the father and daughter were equally matched, but it was the daughter, barely fourteen, who did most of the singing, the father accompanying her on his drum. In the beginning the master preferred the voice of the father, a man over fifty who was growing old, sickly and weak, but soon the master was overcome in amazement by a very special quality in the daughter's proud yet plaintive timbre. All through the autumn the father and his daughter did nothing but sing. Meanwhile, winter was rapidly approaching, and the harsh winds caused the father's already frail health to worsen. Since the beginning of the season his coughs had become more frequent and more severe; finally he could no longer withstand them.

All of a sudden the father began saying that he must leave the household – he had a strange and obstinate insistence.

Because the master could not persuade his guests to stay he let them go, somehow intuiting the old man's intentions, and he said goodbye to the pair. They left the house and disappeared into a street where a fierce wintry wind raged.

Soon afterwards, a rumour reached the household that after wandering about all day the father and daughter had discovered an abandoned hut near the public cemetery and had installed themselves there. They were told that the father had become bedridden and was refusing both food and drink; however, after darkness fell he would sing throughout the night. On hearing these stories the master ordered his servant girl to carry food to the hut.

The proprietress, who was that servant girl, recalled the events clearly. When she reached the hut, carrying the provisions on her head for the pair, everything she saw bore out what she been told. As the villagers listened to the father sing at night they agreed that his songs conveyed feelings of bitter pain and deep despair. They were in accord that since the cemetery had first come into existence they had never heard such mournful tunes. However, no one was disturbed by the father's nightly singing nor did they complain about it. On the contrary, when the villagers looked at the father and daughter they would repress their sighs, the significance of which they themselves could not understand, and muse about the transience of their own lives.

Winter was ending, and it was one of the last days of the lunar year. The night-snow was falling, covering the entire village, hurrying to bury another passing year. During the night, the father sang his last songs in this world, and finally, towards daybreak, he coughed up blood with his final, painful breaths.

The following day the master received word of the death of the father. That evening he sent the servant girl to the hut where the father and daughter had been living. But when the girl arrived she found the villagers returning from the cemetery where they had just buried the body.

After the death of her father, for reasons unknown to the servant girl, the daughter refused to leave the hut. The master wished to bring her once more into his household since she now had no one to look after her, but she stubbornly insisted on remaining there. Not only did she spurn the master's suggestion; she took her dead father's place and began singing his songs. The master was at his wit's end. Unable to persuade her, he sent his servant girl to live with the daughter. What was more, he offered to convert the hut into a small tavern and hired a man to help the two of them run it.

The proprietress continued, 'As a young girl, I had no ear for really fine singing, but I, too, was fascinated by the daughter and her songs. I was most grateful for my master's command and moved in willingly – and that was how I learned to sing. The daughter could no longer refuse the master's kindness, and for a few years she sang for the tavern customers. She did this with great devotion. On the days when there were no customers she would teach me to sing, sometimes late into the night. We lived like that for about three years.' The tavern owner gave the impression that she had just emerged from the haze of a reverie. Slowly and carefully, she continued with her tale.

On the anniversary of her father's death the daughter would prepare fresh purified wine instead of an offering of food as dictated by custom. She placed the wine at the altar of the deceased and sang through the night. One winter's night she sang, this time without the ritual offering of wine, and on the morning after that night of singing she disappeared with the dawn. And she was to be seen no more. It was the third anniversary of her father's death.

The villagers began to talk about the songs that emanated from the tavern. After the father had been buried the daughter had continued his songs, and after her departure the servant girl, now the proprietress, took her place as singer. The villagers refused to believe that the voice they heard belonged to the daughter or to the servant girl. They insisted that it must be that of the long-dead old man; they had no doubt that the soul of his songs, entombed in the grave, was enabling the women to continue to sing in this fashion. To them it did not matter who was the actual singer, the daughter who had disappeared or the servant girl who had taken over the tavern and the songs. The villagers found pleasure in talking about the old man's songs and in confirming their belief in his influence.

'That's how the father's grave came to be called the Song Grave, and the names Song Pass and Song Pass Tavern were coined shortly after this. As for me, I am but a maintainer of his grave. I bear no resentment for my fate, nor do I desire to leave this place. As humble as I am, I have inherited the old man's songs. And as I sing them I wait for the day when someone of his bloodline will pass through this place again. I am truly grateful, for I owe my livelihood to his songs.'

The tavern owner finished her story, her voice punctuated with sighs, and resumed her singing. This time it was a passage from *Hongbo and Nolbu*.[4] She began with Hongbo lamenting his wretched life as a peddler.

At her abrupt opening the man hastily drew the drum towards his breast and, after a few moments' delay, began to accompany her. This time, however, his accompaniment was slow to match the song's enchantment. His face still bore an expression of impatience; the woman's story had left him unsatisfied, his demeanour indicating that he was more preoccupied in delving further into her story than with her music.

Paying no attention to him, she continued to sing, her voice gathering heat and emotion.

Finally, he became aware of a hot flush spreading through his hands and perspiration slowly forming in his palms. As if wandering in the burning valleys of memory, with its flame searing his heart, his eyes ignited with a strange fire while feeling the sun's burning heat. Whenever he listened to a pansori song, the summer sun, this flaming ball of fire, would appear, scorching his body. It was the sun of his childhood, the sun of his fate.

A hillside farm overlooked the sea, where the waves glistened like scales on fish, and sloped up the hill until it reached the border of a camellia grove. A child was tied from his waist to a post at the edge of the farm where an ancient unmarked grave lay near the farm. The farm was the only thing the boy's father had left to his young wife when he died. All summer the boy's mother did nothing but tend the plot of land. Each day, leashed like an animal, the boy endured the long summer's heat. Now and then he would look down at a sailboat gliding over the shimmering sea, breaking the fish-scale waves and disappearing behind an island. At other times he would lie under the searing sun and, feeling hungry, take a midday nap. All the while he would wait for his mother to emerge from the field after finishing her work for the day. Each summer the mother planted soya beans or a mixture of soya and sorghum, and, once inside the furrows of the field, she ignored her son's longing for her. He would see only his mother's bent figure moving in and out of the plants, reminding him of a buoy floating on the water. He would hear a strange voice emanating from her as she worked, a nasal sing-song or moaning sound. Her voice would slowly reach him and then recede into silence. This pattern went on throughout the day.

Then, one day, a peculiar singing voice came from the sloping path overlooking the sea that led from the farm into the mountains. The song it sang was the kind that fuel-woodcutters would sing while crossing a mountain path. But that day no woodcutter could be seen on his way into the mountains, and no one saw the singer. All day the voice came from somewhere in the green shade of the mountains. The villagers later discovered that it was the voice of an itinerant songman who was passing by the village for the first time. The disembodied voice resounded from the forest until sunset. Meanwhile, as she worked in the furrows under the burning sun, the mother's odd moaning, sobbing voice grew more intense and clear and reached out as if in response to the one coming from the mountain path. Finally, the sun began to set behind the mountain peaks, and the opaque shadow of dusk spread itself over the foot of the mountains. It was then that the singing voice made its stealthy descent from the green-shrouded mountains and overcame the boy's mother, still working in between the furrows, like a snake devouring its prey.

The following day the man with the voice entered the village and took up residence in the room next to the gate of the boy's house. Every morning at dawn the songman would return to the mountains, and all day long the villagers would hear him sing, his voice booming like a mountain quake from the depths of the forest. The villagers heard only songs, but in his songs they conjured up an image of the spirit of the forest, cowering, fearing to show its face. At the same time the mother's song grew even more frantic as the days went by. As he lay tied to the ground the child continued to endure the songman's voice. Listening to the songs he would fall asleep, the sleep of hunger, and then he would be awakened by them. Asleep or awake, he could not escape the music swirling in his ears or the sun that hung above him, the flaming ball of fire.

The faceless voice implanted in the boy's memory a face more distinct than the flames of the burning summer sun and doomed him to wander in search of that sun, the face of his fate.

The summer of the songman's arrival had long passed, the new year had swiftly replaced the old, and it was summer again. Yet it was on the morning after his mother had suddenly died and her soul departed from this world that the boy's eyes finally and surely caught sight of the owner of that voice. An unforeseen calamitous event had struck her dead during the night. After suffering a long, horrific, earth-shattering pain, the mother dropped from her womb a bloody mass in the shape of a tiny baby girl. The following morning the mother closed her eyes for ever, and the boy saw the drooping figure of the songman enter the brush gate of their house.

But the boy did not believe that the songman's visage was the real face of the songs. It was the flaming ball of fire that was the true face of the songs, which remained with him even after he had grown into a man.

The death of the boy's mother changed the songman's circumstances, and he could not remain in the village. He was forced to drift from place to place, begging for food with the newborn infant and the boy in tow. Even when the boy accompanied his stepfather as they moved on, the true face of the songs remained the same – the sun.

Anguished and pained as the face was, he could not live without recollecting it. If he did not see the sun and feel its burning heat he felt certain that his flesh and soul would languish, so to this day he was bound to journey inter-minably to seek his encounter with that flaming sun.

Now the traveller encountered that sun once again in the proprietress's songs and found himself still bearing the heat of his fate, pushing his endurance to the limit.

The woman stopped singing; the passage from the *The Song of Hongbo and Nolbu* had come to an end. Yet on the man's face remained the same expression of pain, a pain of perseverance. Streaks of sweat surfaced on his brow and nose like a man exposed to the extreme heat of sun.

'So, am I to understand that you have never heard from her since she left this place?' he asked cautiously, waking from his deep reverie. He drained the wine from the cup to wet his throat and resumed his inquisition, still not quite satisfied with her story. 'Even though she never sent word of her whereabouts, don't you have any idea at all where she was heading?'

The proprietress showed no sign of interest in his continued probing – or, rather, having already fathomed his innermost thoughts, perhaps she was trying to stop herself from being indiscreet. To the questions he put to her she gave no clear response. 'I've already told you that I couldn't guess where she might have gone.'

It was obvious to the man that she was avoiding further conversation.

'If you really don't know, at least you must have heard her mention the name of the place where she and her father had lived before coming here.'

'Don't you see, these itinerant singers never remain in one place. As I understand it they travelled endlessly throughout this southern province.'

'Didn't they have any relatives? I mean, didn't she have any brothers or sisters?'

'We didn't even know where they were born. Do you suppose such people would open their hearts and tell you all about their family history? Even if she had a relative, how could she, a blind woman, attempt to look for that person?'

'No! You mean to say the woman was without sight? What happened? Presumably she wasn't born blind?' His expression became agitated, and he seemed in sudden turmoil.

She ignored his reaction to her careless words, but she continued in a more gentle tone. 'Didn't I mention to you that she was blind? Well, when we were living together, because she was always very orderly and well organized I often forgot that she couldn't see. I believe she was not born blind, as you have guessed.'

'Then how did she lose her sight? What did the people say about how she had become blind? Tell me everything you heard.' His voice trembled from an apprehension he was powerless to control.

'I don't really know the details for sure but . . .' She hesitated, and her eyes showed fear, but she saw that he would not allow her to stop now.

It was none other than her own father who had blinded her. That was the astounding secret the proprietress imparted to him. One night, when the daughter was not yet quite ten years old, she awoke from her sleep in excruciating pain. She felt her face aflame, and her eyes burned like they were on fire. Her father had poured acid into them while she was sleeping next to him, and that was how she had lost her sight. Everyone in the village knew about it, and, as a servant girl, the proprietress had also heard adults talking about it. They said that if the sight were taken away the energy that enabled the eyes to see would be diverted to the ears and throat, empowering the voice to become extraordinary. When the proprietress was still young she did not believe the horrible story. Later, unable to contain her curiosity, she confronted the daughter with her disbelief. The blind woman responded to her questions with deep prolonged sighs, which she understood to mean she should believe the unbelievable.

'But why are you, my dear guest, so interested in gossip such as this?' the proprietress asked the traveller irritably. 'From the beginning I could see that you were more impressed by her story than my songs. I wonder whether you have an especial reason for it,' she said with a hint of spite in her voice.

The guest's demeanour grew rough and uncontrolled, betraying the impression that his long-suppressed premonition was about to become reality. The colouring of his face, too, began to assume a certain unpleasant pallor of indefinable menace. In response to the woman's query he shook his head convulsively.

'Then,' she continued, unaware of the turmoil in the traveller's mind, 'it seems you really believe every word I have said. As for me, I still can't be sure that if one is blinded one can sing better. Do you think it's possible?' she asked abstractedly. Becoming aware of the threatening flash in his eyes as he shook his head, she abruptly ceased talking. She was unable to figure out the nature of the murderous glint in his eyes nor why he shook his head so violently. She could not tell whether he disbelieved that when a person was blinded a voice sang sweeter songs or whether he mistrusted the story of the father–daughter pansori singers altogether. She lacked the insight to read his behaviour, to bore into his mind and comprehend his understanding that the father's true intent was not to endow the daughter with finer voice; rather, he had a motive even more obvious and more cruel. For a long time a deep silence hung heavy between the traveller and the proprietress.

She slowly resumed her singing in a gesture to draw him out and soften the awkwardness in the air. This time, she began with a scene from *The Song of Sim Cheong*,[5] a depiction of the blind man, Sim, on his way to the capital:

> 'O, how we go, o, how we go.
> To the capital we go on a long journey.
> Where shall we rest tonight?
> Where will we sleep tomorrow night?'

The timbre of her voice was lingering, melancholic, in the manner characteristic of *jinyangjo* style of pansori singing. With his eyes half closed the guest accompanied the song. He trailed drowsily behind the woman's singing at times and then suddenly rushed his pace to meet hers. But he was no longer listening to her. On his head he once again felt the flaming summer sun of his childhood and listening to the songs of the songman of long ago, a father to the fatherless boy.

After the death of the boy's mother, the songman took the boy and the infant daughter with him as he moved aimlessly from village to village, peddling his songs in order to feed the half-siblings. In this way almost ten years had passed. All the while the songman had wanted nothing more than to teach the children to sing. The boy, however, had no desire to acquire the skill but went through the motions of learning. So the song-man gave up on the boy and began to teach his daughter, while he taught his stepson to play the drum to accompany her. She was good at mimicking her father's songs, but she must also have been born with talent, for her voice was pleasing. When the father eventually allowed the young children to amuse an audience with their songs he saw that the listeners applauded the novices' fine artistry.

The songman's dearest wish was to train the children to be a brother-and-sister team, but the boy was secretly unwilling to go along with his stepfather's plans. On the contrary, believing it was this man's songs that had killed his mother, he was plotting a scheme to murder him – and his songs with him. He had lived in fear that sooner or later he, too, would be killed by the songman. He was terrified of his stepfather's silent gaze even more, for he had seldom seen him open his mouth except to sing. He longed to comfort his mother's spirit, to free her from the grudges that she had borne and the pain that she had suffered in this world. The boy vowed that he must get rid of his stepfather before his own life was threatened. It was because of this secret plot that the boy could not abandon his stepfather. When he was ordered by the man to play his drum, because he feared for his life he did so obediently, but all the while he waited for a suitable moment. When he listened to the songman's songs, his deliberate and lingering voice, the boy would find himself awake to thoughts of murder. What tormented him beyond endurance was the fireball of the summer sun that would surface in his mind, riding on the songman's chants.

Each time his stepfather sang, the boy felt he was getting closer to accomplishing his murderous plans. Sometimes he would watch the songman slip into a trance induced by his own songs, even when no one was listening. As they travelled on the mountain paths or rested on the empty *maru*[6] of an abandoned hut the songman would slump to the ground and let loose his keening voice. When his singing reached its climax, one could imagine the echoes of his song bouncing off the mountain peaks and causing the birds in the valleys to stop their twittering. At such times the sun of the songman would flame even more fiercely, and uncontrollable thoughts

41

of murdering his stepfather would invade the boy's mind.

The songman's songs created another peculiar effect of sorcery on the child. They had the power simultaneously to stimulate his already treacherous intentions and to sap the energy required to execute them. This left him completely exhausted. No sooner would the boy come close to realizing his plot than the songman's songs would render him powerless, making him feel that the very nerve of his scheme was paralysed by the songs' venomous potion. The child would become lethargic, displaying the symptoms of a strange malaise. More peculiar still was the stepfather's behaviour towards the child. The stepson was quite sure that the songman had somehow divined those secrets he had long been harbouring, and this made him even more fearful of his stepfather. But the songman never betrayed any sign that he was aware of the boy's schemes, although he must surely have suspected them. Either he was oblivious to all else around him, engrossed only in his singing, or it was possible that he had already gauged what was going on in his stepson's mind and was aware of the strange and murderous glint in the boy's eyes whenever he sang. Perhaps it was with this knowledge that he went on singing even more frantically, goading the boy, his voice modulated in deep despair and resignation.

Finally, one autumn afternoon, everything became clear to the boy. The family of three singers was crossing a mountain path in an unfamiliar region. The party proceeded in a leisurely manner while the stepfather continued to sing. The children followed him, leaving in their wake the faint reverberations of their songs. When they reached the top of the mountain the songman stopped and crouched down to the ground, and he resumed his singing in full-throated bursts on this new stage. The mountains were ablaze with autumnal hues, and the distant valleys were shrouded in an opaque, milky haze. The songman's lengthy rendition continued, and it was as though nature resonated with his songs in an expression of the *han*, a fateful, insoluble anguish – unremitting regret and unrequited grudges – that had been embedded in the soul of his people. Finally, exhausted by the emotional weight of his songs, he lay on a cushion of fallen leaves piled up by the wayside and appeared to fall asleep.

The boy had listened to his stepfather's songs of despair and again became affected by the same peculiar, languid sensation, the energy drained from his body. Deep sighs doubled him up, and he trembled. He could not bear it any longer. But then a strange sorrow pushed upwards from his heart, empowering him with an incomprehensible energy. He slowly collected his strength, shook himself out of his stupor and began to circle the songman.

But the man was not asleep. Clasping a large stone to his breast, the boy approached his stepfather. Not even his little half-sister had noticed his approach. The boy stood there for a long time, frozen by his own fear, wishing desperately for his stepfather to wake up and catch him in the act. At that very moment the songman raised his head and took a long look at his stepson.

'Why are you standing there like that?' he asked, his voice betraying a hint of irritation that suggested that he had been kept waiting for too long. But he left things at that and did not ask about the rock that he was holding. After challenging the boy the songman returned to his position of feigned sleep, almost taunting the boy, who was mystified by this behaviour.

He could not bear to be near the sleeping man any longer. The songman had ignored the child who had approached him with a stone clutched to his chest. The songman must have read the youth's mind, but why had he assumed an ignorance of his intent? This question remained in the boy's mind, a riddle to which he could find no answer.

That afternoon the boy finally left his stepfather. He dropped the stone and started walking towards the woods, pretending he needed to urinate. He disappeared for ever from the sight of the father and the daughter. As the boy emerged out of the woods, far away from his kin, he could hear the song-man calling him, his voice echoing from the distant valley. He pictured the songman racing about in search of him and hastened his step in the opposite direction. Since that day he could find no place on earth where he could escape from the songman's call. In every pansori song he heard, anywhere and at any time, his stepfather's calls pursued him.

Nothing had changed since that autumn day. Once again in the proprietress's song the traveller listened to the desper-ate shouts of his stepfather, and once again he heard his own laboured breathing as he ran from that cry.

'Why don't you stop for a while and rest your voice.' The traveller was exhausted by his own reverie, and when he inter-rupted the proprietress his suggestion was not just for the singer.

His face was completely drained of life. 'So what did the daughter tell you about the cruel father who blinded her?' he asked after downing a few cups of wine. His voice was calm again.

'She never talked about it.' The proprietress had become gentler in her manner, most likely realizing that there was nothing more to hide from him.

'Even if she said nothing, didn't you wonder whether she had forgiven her father – perhaps by watching how she behaved towards him?'

To fend off his persistent questions she was evasive in her response. 'Since she never talked about it and showed no resentment, I supposed she might have forgiven him. Those who know a thing or two about pansori tell me that what the father did was entirely just and even admirable.'

'You mean by blinding his daughter in order to improve her singing?'

'They say in order to train a singer to produce fine songs, the voice must experience indescribable pain.'

'Is that the reason why the father took sight from his own daughter's eyes, in order for her to experience in her heart this *han*?'

'So I have heard people say,' the proprietress assured the man.

'No, I don't believe it,' he replied. 'This *han* you talk about, this unremitting suffering, unavenged wrongs, this belief in an undeserved fate inflicted upon us – this can neither be taught nor passed on. Little by little, like dust, it accumulates throughout one's lifetime. Some people live to acquire this *han* and amass it in order to live. Perhaps it is disrespectful to the memory of the father who is no longer of this world – and I am sorry to have to say this – but I have a feeling it was not just for her songs that he blinded his daughter. I believe he did so to prevent her from running away from him.'

No words came from the woman. The traveller paid no attention. He no longer cared whether she understood what he was talking about. He rambled on in a hazy monologue that came from the depths of his meditation. 'Anyway, it was good that she forgave her father, for him and for her. If she had not been able to forgive him she would have been left only with vengeful hatred but never a *han* that would enhance her singing power. It is because of her redeeming act of forgiveness that she was able to experience the depth of the *han*.'

'I gather you feel at peace only if you so believe.' She smiled for the first time. Finally trusting the traveller, she asked unabashedly, 'So, now that you know the daughter was blinded will you keep on looking for your half-sister?'

He did not seem perturbed by her sudden revelation. 'If I could yet hope, I wish to find her songs, even if only for a moment and from afar. But I wonder if such a day will ever come.' He spoke in a calm, casual voice but wondered how she could have read his thoughts. A hint of curiosity flashed in his eyes as he looked at her.

She had already sensed what was in the traveller's mind, but, betraying nothing, and with an air of innocence, she disclosed her last piece of information. 'I remember her mentioning a brother who accompanied her on his drum as a child. Did I forget to tell you about him?'

THE LIGHT OF SONGS

THE TAVERN CROUCHED on the banks of a bend in the mean-dering Tamjingang River, about four kilometres from the town of Janghung. A tree-lined rural bus route linked Janghung and neighbouring Gangjin. From the river bend one could see the rocky mist-shrouded summit of Eokbulsan Mountain, known as a landmark, some four kilometres away. On either side of the bus route along the river a dozen or so thatched houses huddled together, and the tavern stood a little further down the road, closer to the river. It was a tavern in name only, for not many travellers frequented this rural road, and the owner could hardly make ends meet with only the occasional customer stopping by.

A man by the name of Cheon ran the tavern – the third generation of his family to do so – which did not even have a sign to indicate its business. The fish Cheon caught from the river were the main source of the tavern's income. One day, when he was already past thirty, a young woman had strayed into his tavern, and they ended up spending the night together like a married couple on their wedding night. But the following morning this woman he had hoped would remain his bride for the rest of his life ran away with a bundle containing the contents of all his furniture drawers. From that day he remained unmarried until he was over fifty. In all seasons Cheon would go down to the river to fish, just as his forefathers had done before him. Then he would go into town and sell his fish to various bars there, which used them as side dishes to accompany drink. And so he managed to keep his tavern going.

He was not the only resident of the tavern, however. There was another, a not-quite-ordinary woman of about thirty years old who was blind and who took care of the place when Cheon went to the river to fish. She received and served the customers and managed general chores, acting like the proprietress in the man's absence. Although unable to see, she was perfectly capable of handling all his responsibilities and, in fact, appeared to be entirely comfortable doing them.

Although there was almost never a whisper of gossip about why they were living together, one might have wondered why she was there. Why would a blind woman, of all people, be working in this humble tavern? In the beginning some speculated that the ageing bachelor Cheon had lured the blind woman to the tavern to be his wife, thinking she would not run away because she could not see. Yet, after about ten years had passed since her arrival, the villagers, when they detected nothing illicit in the relationship, ceased to speculate. Still, some of the neighbours whispered that Cheon was impotent. Both the blind woman and Cheon, however, conducted themselves as if impervious to the gossip. She had never spoken to anyone about the details of her life, and he turned a deaf ear to enquiries about her. To avoid facing the villagers Cheon would go to the river alone at dawn and fish all day up and down the stream. As for the blind woman, all she did during this time was serve the infrequent customers – which she did in silence – or come out of the tavern and crouch under the awning on the *maru* and cast her sightless eyes in the direction of the distant mountains, assuming the posture of one who is waiting for something.

Sometimes, after the sun had set and Cheon had returned from the river, when the night had deepened and there was no need to wait for customers, utterly enchanting songs, songs peculiar to the southern provinces, could be heard drifting out from a corner room of the tavern. It would be so late that the dozen or so families near by would be fast asleep, and even if there were some sleepless souls among them they would have barely been able to hear the woman's songs. And if some passers-by chanced to overhear them, they would surely shrug their shoulders, cock their heads and move on, dismissing the songs as nothing more than an impotent man's strange and solitary nocturnal game.

One early evening on a late autumn day, a stranger to the region entered the tavern. He had been walking in a leisurely manner along the bus route from town, enjoying the sight of the persimmon trees that reached over the dirt walls of the thatched dwellings, their branches gracefully arched under the weight of the fully ripened fruits of the frosty season. His weary expression made him look ten years older than his actual age of around forty. He told the people that, as a collector of medicinal herbs for a traditional pharmaceutical concern in Seoul, he travelled throughout the country collecting ingredients. However, his coming to this tavern did not seem to be by chance. In the village he had not talked with the locals about herbs nor enquired about where he might find them. He had the air of a man who knew exactly where he was headed, one who had already made up his mind to spend the night at the tavern. Indeed, as he approached it he had the expression of someone already savouring the effect of drink.

Furthermore, there was something out of the ordinary in the traveller's behaviour when he faced the blind woman who greeted him. His aspect did not betray any discomfort or surprise that the woman who served him was blind. On the contrary, he showed a hint of relief, as if he had expected to be met by such a woman – or perhaps this blind woman's calm, self-composed demeanour had soothed his weariness and induced in him a state of tender repose. Perched on the *maru* of the tavern, he went on drinking cup after cup of wine, occasionally letting his tentative gaze linger on the woman's profile. At last there was nothing else to occupy him.

'How about it? Would you let me hear some of your songs tonight?' the traveller asked late in the evening, after the gathering chill of the autumn night had forced him to move into a room where the woman continued to serve him wine. Cheon had already returned from the river, and it was after she had taken a dinner table into Cheon's room.

'It is not by chance that I am here,' he volunteered. 'I have heard of you from the people in town. There is nowhere in the south where I have not been to seek good songs. Fine wines are not what I am after. Would you sing for such a man? I would gladly sit the whole night here if you would sing for me.' Unlike his previous tone of indifference, there was an intensity in his pleading voice when he said this, and it was easy to tell from his aspect that he was clearly a man worn down by many years as a vagabond.

Since her arrival at the tavern the blind woman had received requests to sing from only one or two customers a year. Yet, instead of being grateful for the traveller's request, a rare opportunity to profit from her singing, she allowed a flash of anger pass across her face, as though she were being trifled with, made to feel like a plaything. But all at once she understood that she could not refuse the request. When he begged her to sing for a second time, she felt her displeasure slowly give way to deep resignation, and, as she cast her sightless gaze on the man she could not see, her face began to wear a strange, pensive expression of foreboding.

She agreed to sing late in the evening, when the stillness brought the sound of the river's surge even closer through the window. She walked backwards and forwards between her room and Cheon's several times to see whether he needed anything more. When she came back, the traveller noted that there was a change in her appearance; she had rearranged her hair and adorned herself with a traditional costume of a short blouse and a long flowing skirt. She reached up to a shelf and gently took down to her bosom a worn drum and a drumstick. She began:

> 'From Hampyeong's heaven and earth
> To my birthplace, Gwangju, I wish to return.
> This old man, I go,
> Borrowing a boat in Jeju Island
> To cross the sea of Haenam.'

This was 'The Song of Honam', a *tan-ga*[7] popular among the southerners. She accompanied herself on the drum with lingering rhythmic beats. From the opening strains, she sang in a powerfully commanding voice:

> 'The sun rising from Heungyag shines on Boseong
> The morning mist shrouding Mount Kosan
> Spreads towards Yeongam.'

What emerged from her throat did not sound like a woman's voice at all. The voice had the quality of the mournful and pain-laden tone characteristic of southern songs, yet with her hoarse vocal timbre it resembled more the full-throated throbbing lamentation of a heroic man percolating from a soul's depths than a beautiful woman's musing on a frosty moonlit autumn night, reminiscent of the distant cry of geese in flight.

No expression of bewilderment appeared on the traveller's face while he listened with his eyes closed. He found himself resonating with her masculine singer's voice, seduced by its bold manner of expression which defied her femininity. He nodded repeatedly in acknowledgement and in response and slipped deeper and deeper into a trancelike intoxication. Only after she had finished did he finally open his eyes.

'Excellent. Excellent indeed!' With this sincere compliment he handed the wine cup to the performer so that she could soothe her throat. He begged for more. The singer accepted the cup with both hands and drained it reverentially. She handed the cup back to him and, her mind already made up, prepared without a moment's hesitation to start another song:

> 'Nay, nay,
> What use are the things of this world . . .
> Have you seen a paradise on earth?'

She continued in her strong and solemn voice, and again he drank in the sound of her song with his eyes closed and moving his head to the rhythm. Her song gathered strength, and as it simmered with passion, its heat drew beads of perspiration on her face. On the listener's face a shadow of suffering became visible. His brow furrowed in an endurance of pain, and his breathing grew rougher. He, too, was sweating.

> 'Our life nothing but a passing spring dream.
> Have a drink of wine, and let us be merry.'

When she had concluded an elegant passage from 'Pyeon-sichun' – a *tan-ga* about an ephemeral spring dream – the traveller handed the wine cup to her and urged her over and over to continue. He was growing impatient with her *tan-ga*; this fragmentary singing with frequent pauses for breath hardly satisfied him.

When the singer had concluded another *tan-ga* with considerable effort, the traveller made a request. 'I suppose you are ready for a real song, now that you have warmed up with your *tan-ga*. How about *Chunhyang-ga* or *Sim Cheong-ga* – anything your heart desires, any passage from them – I mean?' He was now requesting her to sing pansori.

However, she was already exhausted – but not from singing songs in preparation for the pansori; she no longer cared whether she had any strength left to go on. As she had become aware that the guest's breathing was growing increasingly harsh as he listened, she felt a strange flash of foreboding in her sightless eyes, and finally it immobilized all her movements.

'You have such a deep desire for songs?'

No answer came from the man. He flinched, suspecting she had read his mind. He recovered himself and fixed his sight on her. It was obvious that she did not wish to continue; she needed to rest her voice.

'I wonder why you have come to enjoy listening to songs so much. I have never met a lover of pansori who does not have a reason for becoming one.' The singer spoke with conviction.

'What do you mean by "a reason"?' He hesitated for a moment, then took a deep breath, struggling to speak. Finally, he decided what he should say. 'If you ask why I have become so obsessed with songs, there is something in my life that you might think is the cause of it.'

His expression remained withdrawn. When he spoke

again, it was in a hollow voice. 'Yes, there is a reason. I am over forty now and looking wretched. I have been everywhere in this region hoping to find songs. But tonight, meeting your voice this way, I know that all the days of wandering were worth while. I have no regrets.'

'My humble songs do not deserve to be heard,' the singer demurred.

A hint of a smile surfaced on his lips as he shook his head. 'Don't deny it. There is something delightful and precious in your voice, something I value and cherish above anything I have ever known in my life. I feel that it is for this very dear thing – more than for the songs – that I have searched in vain all my life.'

'What is it? What is so very precious and valuable to you?' She was becoming increasingly agitated and anxious.

'If you care to listen, I will tell you.'

He began. It was the same story he had recounted years before to the proprietress of Song Pass Tavern in Boseong after he had listened to her songs all through the night. It was the remembrance of a flaming summer sun, a ball of fire that was lost with his childhood and beginning to fade from his memory. Anywhere, anytime he listened to a pansori song, the traveller experienced the heat of that sun beating down on him, the sun of his fate scorching his face and lashes.

The man concluded his story calmly, as if it belonged to someone else. 'My mother died when a bloody lump of flesh in the shape of an infant dropped from her womb, and my step-father, the songman, could no longer remain in the village. He buried the infant's mother and left the village with the infant.' The boy did not believe the songman's face was the face of the songs, but the flaming sun remained in his consciousness as the true face of the songs. A suffering, pain-ridden face though it was, he could not live a day without it – without feeling its burning heat, his body and soul wasted away. It was in search of this sun of his fate that he had wandered half his life.

'I needn't go on telling you what happened to me after that time. You can well imagine the rest. In any event, I have been drifting ever since. Yet I am unable to rid myself of the miserable memory of my childhood. I go from place to place, a god-forsaken beggar of songs. Whenever I listen to pansori singing an image surfaces in my mind of the breaking ocean waves I watched as a child from the soya-bean patch, glistening like fish scales, and I can feel the wind on my face from the deep forest, that cool breeze rising after a short summer rain, washing away the sultry heat. And, more significantly, I see once again the same scorching summer sun that hovered over me with such a horrific intensity that it singed my eyelashes. I tell you now. What I mean is that in your song I meet that sun. Never have I encountered a song that holds a sun as powerful as yours. Now you must understand why I have been so drawn to them.' Even after he had finished his story his face remained twisted in pain like a man suffering in the sun's intense heat.

The woman's expression had betrayed no sign of the turmoil in her mind until the traveller's story came to an end. She sat immobile, desolate, her sightless eyes fixed on the void, her figure bent, exhausted and lifeless like a withered roadside tree under the summer sun, just as when she would come outside and crouch under the tavern's awning and, turning her empty gaze towards nothing in particular, endlessly wait for something. When the guest had concluded his story the glimmer of a vague foreshadowing that had spun about in her sightless eyes had disappeared completely, leaving no trace.

'Very well, then, I'll let you listen to me sing all night.' She spoke in an effort to soothe him. She adjusted her sitting position and then silently pushed towards him the drum and the drumstick she had been holding against her chest, an indication that if he wanted to listen to her songs he must be willing to accompany her. This was her habit when her customers asked her to sing, and she always trusted their hands.

The man seemed to shrink away from her, his eyes clearly showing confusion as he looked at the instruments thrust at him. But her blank eyes pursued him, allowing him no alternative but to accept her terms.

'I haven't touched the drum for so long. I wonder whether my accompaniment can match your songs.' But he realized he could not resist her gesture and drew the instruments slowly to him. And so began the duet of the blind woman and the traveller which promised to last the whole night.

The traveller was now swept into the vortex of her pansori singing. She began with the depiction of a ghost with a head of wormwood stalk. She then switched to Chunhyang's prison elegy, which she followed with Hongbo's lamentation of his sad lot as a peddler. With each song her performance remained faithful to the various styles of the celebrated master pansori singers of the region.[8] She concluded with a scene re-enacting the blind man Sim's sorrowful journey to the capital.

The blind songstress showed no sign of fatigue. She sang in a hoarse, masculine voice in the *u-jo* tradition, which was at the same time delicately shaded with a crystalline elegance characteristic of the feminine *kyemyeon-jo* mode. At times the grandeur of her voice thundered, conjuring up images of magnificent mountain crags. At other times the voice imparted an illusion of sorrow, the sound of a falling petal or of other-worldliness, the chilly shiver of an autumn frost. The voice led the listener beyond a breathtaking precipice to a slow meandering river that coursed through valleys and endless fields. It invoked a fierce stormy night followed by afternoon meadows bursting into flower and birds twittering mellifluously in their midst.

The traveller mirrored the songstress's superb artistry with his own. Whenever she finished a passage, she would ask him what she should sing next. 'How about Chunhyang's prison song?' or 'How about Hongbo's lamentation over his wretched lot.'

He would take up her suggestions gladly. At her prompting he would beat the drum in rhythmic sympathy with her song. At any tempo he would follow her song as effortlessly as if he had memorized it by heart. Neither the singer nor the drummer betrayed a trace of surprise at the other's artistry. Single-mindedly, they kept up their performance.

> O, how we go. O, how we go
> To the capital, ten thousand li, how we go.
> Where shall we rest tonight?
> Where shall we sleep tomorrow night?
> Slowly feeling our way, we go without a destination
> In the season of midsummer,
> The sunrays, the sparks from flaming fire.
> And sweat flows like rain.

Her singing was a harmonious blending of ever-varying tonal qualities. At times her voice rolled and trilled, at other times stalled and then gradually unravelled. Gently skimming the surface of the drum accompaniment and weaving between the beats with consummate skill, the voice enticed the drummer, allowing him more and more pleasure in his own playing. The duet of the song and drum was an exquisite, perfect embrace in which one never touched the other, like a courtesan's tantalizing art of giving pleasure without a caress. It was more than a temptress's teasing; it was an act of breath-taking sorcery.

Even in their embrace there was no surprise. Only the man's tortured face began to transform, sweat breaking out, and once again he met the sun of his childhood, endured once more that terrible heat. He panted from the heat and struggled to stifle the heavy sound of his breathing. As for the singer, it was as though she so passionately desired to intensify the heat and pain of the flame blazing over the drummer's head that she willingly sang until daybreak. Finally, at dawn, the man and the woman lay down side by side in her room. She had had customers who, after listening to her songs, wished to sleep with her. Cheon had not minded what went on during the night between the woman and her customers; he did not seem to regard such things as indecent.

There was no need for words between the singer and the traveller as they lay together. They expressed no surprise. From the start both had foreknowledge of what would come to pass, and so had been prepared. When the sun rose the traveller left the tavern quietly, without a word. This, too, they took as pre-ordained.

On the bedding there was no trace of the night's occupant. When the woman awoke from her slumber, she caressed the empty space next to her and, gently, with the utmost care, rolled up the bedding and put it away. Then, deliberately, she opened the door and came out of her room. Cheon, seated on the *maru*, was waiting for her, enveloped in the rays of the late morning sun that had already crept deep into the middle of the space.

'Has the guest gone on his way?' Cheon asked.

With her empty eyes the woman searched beyond the

fields to the distant mountains and spoke abstractedly, as if to herself. 'It happened so. My brother left without a word.'

'Your brother? The traveller of last night?' Cheon questioned with a sudden show of concern.

'Yes. I met my half-brother last night.' Her voice and expression betrayed no agitation.

Cheon made a wide nodding movement but pressed her further. 'I had a feeling that something odd was going on last night, but I never heard you say you had a brother before now. You mean to tell me that the infant was you? That baby born to the woman working in the soya field, impregnated by that voice from the mountains, that was you?' Cheon's question was straightforward. He made no effort to conceal the fact that he had eavesdropped on the conversation between her and the traveller the night before.

'It is indeed so.' Her answer was clear, and her manner suggested that there was nothing further to hide from him.

'But to the end my brother could not bring himself to say that the bloody new-born flesh was a girl. He never mentioned that he himself went on the road with the songman when he left the village holding the infant. He tried to talk about things that are beyond my recall, things that I could never have remembered. Still, I recollect well enough.' Calmly, she revealed to Cheon as many of the stories of her childhood as she could recall. She began by telling him how her songman father had gone from place to place singing for food with the half-siblings in tow. The sole wish of the father as they moved had been to teach the children to sing. He trained them strictly, these children who were not yet old enough to understand the circumstances of their lives. She reflected on the song-man's constant training during their travels. The half-siblings seldom enjoyed respite from his single-minded efforts to teach them. The father instructed them even when they were forced to stop on their mountain trek, fatigued, or while living in a storage shed of an abandoned house where they had taken temporary shelter. For some unknown reason the brother adamantly refused to learn, but the sister responded well. Eventually, as they travelled, the brother learned to accompany his half-sister, to embellish her singing. The villagers of the region began to talk about the brother-and-sister team. Throughout everything, however, the brother remained unhappy, even as the accompanist of her songs. One autumn day, when they had stopped to rest on a deserted mountain path, he ran away. While the songman lay stretched out on the ground, exhausted from singing a passage from *Water Palace Song*, the brother disappeared into the woods – just like that.

'After my brother left', the blind woman resumed, 'the songman began to worry that the girl might run away, too. So that is the reason why he blinded his own daughter.' At last she had disclosed to Cheon the cause of her blindness.

After the girl had lost her sight the light in her eyes was reborn in her vocal chords and bestowed upon her voice a rich lustre. The effect of this transformation enabled the father and daughter to support themselves comfortably as itinerant singers. Then, one winter's evening, the songman died in an abandoned hut near the town of Boseong – but not before he had imparted to his daughter the secret that he had always kept to himself. Foreseeing that an illicit relationship might develop between the half-siblings, he had put poison in her eyes while she slept next to him. The songman departed from this world weeping, begging forgiveness from his daughter for his transgressions.

Cheon, who had been silent until this point, objected, his face still bearing a disturbed expression. 'Even if you had a half-brother, how can you be sure that last night's guest was him? As I see it, neither one of you disclosed your true identity.'

'When I first confronted the traveller, I felt he might be my half-brother. When he told me why he had journeyed far and wide seeking songs, I did not doubt him, so that when I handed him the drum and drumstick to him, and when my song met his drumbeat, I had to suppress the word *brother* that welled up inside me. He played the drum the same way the songman, my father, had played it.'

'Then the man you call your brother must have recognized you as his half-sister.'

'I am inclined to think so.' Her voice remained calm and sure as she continued. 'And he came looking for me, knowing where I was. That's what I think. Even if he had come without knowing who I was, I am sure he knew when he started playing the drum.'

'Then, I wonder, assuming he recognized you, why he left without saying a word about your relationship.'

'I think it was because he wanted to kill me, too.'

'What! Your half-brother wanted to kill you?' Cheon's eyes widened.

'There was one more thing my father revealed before he died. He told me that every time he sang he saw a murderous gleam in my brother's eyes. As my father watched the heat rising in his stepson's eyes he could feel that the boy was tortured by the desire to harm him. He also knew why my brother travelled with him reluctantly. My father realized that he believed that he, my wretched father, had killed his mother, and he wanted more than anything to avenge her death. Knowing these things, my father kept on singing – in fact, even more intensely than before, perhaps to make it easier for my brother to fulfil his desire. Yet, in the end, his stepson chose to run away, unable to carry out his secret plot of revenge. Ultimately my brother was defeated by the songman's songs.

'Last night, when I was singing, I, too, experienced clearly that same flash of destructive energy emanating towards me from the traveller. He said that it was something like a flaming ball of sun, but I know it was the same murderous impulses my father had talked about. When he felt the heat of the sun on his forehead as he listened to my songs, the traveller understood that the old killer instinct was again engulfing him.'

'Why then did you continue to sing with him all night – and with so much devotion? To stir him so that you could bring it to an end? Was that it?'

She remained silent.

'And if your brother felt that raging impulse while listening to your songs, why did he walk out of the gate without harming you, I wonder.'

'It was the same as before. He could not kill my father. He only wished to do so. It was, as he had said, because of the songs that he had to run away. Once more he must have experienced that same murderous energy rising in him as he listened to my singing, and once more he had to leave because of them.'

'Do you think he knew what you were thinking? I mean, was he aware that you sensed his emotions?'

'I know he came to understand it when our playing blended.'

Cheon had not allowed her to pause to reflect, but his persistent questioning finally ceased.

It was her turn to speak. Her voice sounded hollow as she resumed. 'There is one more thing that he knew before he came here. He knew how I had lost my eyesight; he did not have to ask about it. Anyone who sings pansori or who has an ear for pansori and really understands it senses these things – the way, in ten years, you never asked me for the details of my life, all the while allowing me to stay with you like this.'

'Yes. It is true that when I hear you sing I don't need to ask questions about you.' Cheon gained the courage to continue. But now, as he began to speak haltingly, his voice was parched by grief. 'I don't know too much about songs, as your brother does, but I encounter the deep *han* of our existence in your songs, and I can almost picture in my mind's eye all that you have endured in your life. Your sightlessness speaks for itself.' He went on, now in a comforting and sure voice, as if to caress her mind's wounds and assuage her pain. 'I think now he left you in order not to disturb the *han* in your songs. There are people who carry within them this *han* and cherish it like some precious property. They chip away at it, sliver by sliver, and feed themselves with it in order to live. You, for one, I myself and, as far as I know, your half-brother are some of the people I mean. For such people *han* becomes a source of strength and food for life. There is no need to regret having it. *Han* enables a singer of pansori like you to uncover the core of the songs and deepen the voice. So you must cherish and value it all the more. Your brother must have been thinking of this, so I believe. You told me just a while ago that you think your brother left you because he was aware he would be unable to control his impulse to harm you if he had stayed. Even if this is true, I think I am right in supposing that it was because he valued your *han* so much, because he so much wished to leave it undisturbed. I have no doubt that he left in order to prevent himself from robbing you of it.'

Tears began to form in the woman's sunken eyes and soon began to flow, but Cheon did not notice them. 'Don't feel so sad. It is possible that some day he will return to you,' Cheon said, trying to comfort her.

'I don't think that will ever happen.' Gently, she shook her head. 'He, like me, lives only by his *han*. I know he will never come back to me, for if he did it would rid him of his *han* as well as mine. I know for sure he would not do anything that would waste his *han*.' She then said something entirely unexpected. 'Even if he should return to seek me out, everything has ended. From this moment forth, we, the two half-siblings, must never face one another again.'

Startled by this enigmatic pronouncement Cheon stared at the blind woman. But she had already made up her mind when she went on. 'Just as he holds my songs precious, I have to fulfil my obligation to honour his *han*, which is as valuable to me as it is to him.'

Once more her face was expressionless, with the same empty stare she was in the habit of directing towards the distant mountains.

She had become oblivious to her surroundings, even to the presence of Cheon, who by now was shaking with a grief that defied expression.

She mumbled, more to herself that to him, 'Let me see. It has been already more than ten years since I arrived here and lived with you, dear sir. When I reflect on my lot, I know I have been living an easy life for too long, one I hardly deserve. I think the time has come for me to move on . . .'

IMMORTAL CRANE VILLAGE

AFTER A STOPOVER in the city of Jangheung the bus sped along the perilously narrow road that ran close by the sea. After about an hour it finally reached Hoejin, its final stop. It was late in the afternoon, and the pale autumn sun lingered. As the bus pulled into the terminal the few remaining passengers hastily arose. The young driver opened the emergency exit next to the driver's seat and, alighting from the bus, shook the dust of the road from his head and clothes.

The last person to disembark was a man. The other passengers rushed towards the connecting Wando Island ferry, which was moored at the pier, the sound of the ship's engine urging them to hurry. But this traveller was not in a rush; he had no need to catch the boat. He paused to study the sea beyond the pier. The tide was coming in. He looked like a man with nothing else to do. Then a pharmacy caught his eye, and he hastened towards it as if he had just remembered something. Inside, a young woman was sitting, her face faintly illuminated by rays of the thin afternoon sun. He bought a bottle of Bacchus[9] from her, and said, 'I believe high tide comes in the evening this time of year.'

'I should think so. The fifteenth of the month by the lunar calendar was just a couple of days ago. It's nearly time for high tide now,' she responded lazily. She spoke absent-mindedly, in a local southern accent, as she handed him his change.

'Do you know a place in Immortal Crane Village where I

can spend the night? I remember that a long time ago there used to be a tiny tavern by the roadside.'

Only then did the woman regard the traveller. She noticed that he looked around fifty, but she soon lost interest in him, a shabby-looking man wearing an expression of profound fatigue. She spoke reluctantly. 'So you have been to Immortal Crane Village before. Why shouldn't there be a place for a traveller to stay overnight? It's a village after all, isn't it? The tavern is still there on the way to the village, as far as I know.'

The traveller twisted the cap off the bottle, gulped down the contents and left the shop, urging his heavy feet along as he walked into the street by the wharf and headed towards Immortal Crane Village. To the west the sun still hung a hand's span above the summit of the mountains.

'If I hurry, I can make it,' he muttered to himself.

Thirty years ago, was it? If his recollection was correct, the distance between the Hoejin pier to the village was over four kilometres. He told himself that it didn't matter whether or not he arrived before sunset. If the tavern still existed, he could stop there, and from the tavern he would be able to view the village across the water. If not, he would be satisfied if he could reach as far as the top of the hill from where he could catch sight of the village. All he needed was to be able to see the village before sunset.

The traveller took each step with increased urgency. The road, which had followed the water's edge, gradually began to slope upwards, coursing through rocky hills to the mountain. Beyond the mountain was the village. On the left the hilly trail overlooked the aquamarine water surrounding the Hoejin pier and meandered for some distance along mountain curves lush with pine groves. Although a cooling wind rustled through the pine branches, sweat broke out on the traveller's forehead as he pressed on. He caught sight of a passenger boat sailing smoothly on the water like a scene in a painting. It was about to head out from the pier towards Wando Island. The boat's whistle was a reminder to the man that he must hurry, and, as if he were racing along with the vessel, he walked even more briskly along the snaking mountain road.

But there was no contest between the man and the boat. It had already slipped from the pier into the open sea and begun to disappear behind the island. He was about to round the last bend. In front of his eyes he could see the entrance to a pass through the rocky ridge that would take him to Immortal Crane Village. He grew tense. Viewed from high up on the mountain the sun appeared higher in the sky than when he had seen it from the pier. He anticipated that climbing one more spur would take him to a place where, to his right, he might clearly see the long inlet that cut into the village. And he would also see a spectacle: he would behold the peak of Gwaneumbong Mountain, Mountain of Bodhisattva of Mercy. If he was lucky he might also hear the throbbing drumbeats of the mountain spirit riding on the tide. If he was luckier still he could listen to the remainder of a sorrowful tale of a woman who had vanished without a trace.

Gwaneumbong Mountain, which resembled the shape of an enlightened monk in a meditation pose, was behind the village. The village should probably have been named Gwaneumbong Village, yet it was called Immortal Crane Village, and there was a good reason for this. It was because of the mountain's reflection on the water at high tide in the shape of a flying crane. The soaring mountain crest – the monk's peaked hat – resembled a crane's head at the moment of taking flight. The gently rippling ridges – the monk's robe – were its wings. When the seawater filled the inlet at high tide one could hear the mystical rumblings of the earth spirit that emanated from the heart of the mountain. The sound, audible throughout the area, spread over the water and reached all the way towards the rocky ridge on other side of the inlet, creating an illusion of a monk beating a drum, allowing the villagers to behold the vision of a crane flying over the water.

The village was encircled by the chest of the flying crane. This was how the village came to be known as Immortal Crane Village. No wonder the village was considered propitious. From ancient times it had been said that the most auspicious grave sites were to be found somewhere in the strip of land from which the earth spirit's rumblings were believed to emanate, and all the villagers wished to locate a sacred place there to bury the bones of their ancestors so that their progeny would be blessed with the mountain's yin virtue, that of hidden benevolence. The number of bones buried there were, indeed, beyond counting.

The traveller's steps began to slow down under the burden of unendurable anticipation, but he had no time to waste. He took a deep breath to ease the tension, and he began the ascent of the final spur with long strides.

But as he confronted the scene that was revealed before him his face twisted in confusion. Beyond the rocky ridge he ought to have seen a branch of the sea wedged deeply into the village, but where there should have been water there was none. Instead, between the foot of the rocky ridge and the edge of the right slope of Gwaneumbong Mountain, a dam had been constructed, and it was holding the sea back from the inlet. What had once been the inlet was now farmland that had lately been harvested. In the distance, beyond the field dotted with clusters of farmhouses, Immortal Crane Village came into view.

But now he found no image of a soaring crane, with no prospect of hearing the throbbing drumbeats of the mountain spirit riding the water from the heart of Gwaneumbong Mountain. Only the mountain remained unchanged, still in the shape of a meditating, reverent monk. But now that the water was gone the mountain no longer represented the warmth and compassion of the earth spirit. It was nothing more than an ordinary mountain range with ordinary fields spread out at its feet.

The traveller slumped to the ground, his expectations shattered.

Where there was no water to mirror the mountain, the crane could not fly. Gwaneumbong Mountain was now nothing but a fallen bird with its wings broken, a mountain bereft of its legend.

The traveller saw everything beginning to fade in the advancing dusk. In the last glow of twilight the mountain surfaced beyond the field, empty and desolate, receding gradually from his sight. The wind whistled through the pine branches, gathering in the darkness.

He raised himself from his seat and let his gaze survey the field where the greyness of the approaching evening had begun to spread. Even the village itself had changed beyond recognition. Any hope of hearing news of the woman vanished from his mind. There was no reason why she should want to return to the village where she would find no flying crane. It was already late in the day, and he decided to stay the night at the tavern.

It was not difficult to find it – it was just as easy as the woman in the shop had said it would be. As he emerged from the mountain pass he observed a new hamlet at the foothill of the pine grove, a scattering of around a dozen houses. He suspected that this must have come into existence when the inlet was drained and the land turned into farms. He began to descend with feeble steps. The tavern lay at the entrance to the hamlet, its weatherbeaten shrunken structure crouched like a dried-up mushroom. Its thatched roof remained unchanged, the same one he recalled dimly in his memory, but as he pushed open its brush gate he entered to find a gloomy run-down place.

'Is the tavern-keeper here?'

When the traveller had made his presence known, a middle-aged woman emerged from the dimly lit kitchen, wiping water from her hands with the edge of her wraparound skirt. At first, he could not recollect her face and wondered if the tavern had changed hands. But then he recalled that the keeper of the tavern had been past fifty. The traveller remembered the saying 'Ten years can change the aspects of mountains and rivers' – meaning there had been time enough to alter the appearance of nature three times – so he reasoned that the changes that had taken place in the village were to be expected. And there was no reason to believe that the same old man would be the tavern-keeper.

'I'd like something to drink,' the traveller demanded peremptorily.

'Do you want wine?' the woman responded. She didn't sound especially welcoming.

'I don't mind,' he replied half-heartedly. He slumped and sat on the *maru*.

'It might not be quite to your liking. It might not taste especially good because I've had it for a few days. I assume that's all right with you,' the woman informed him, sounding reluctant to serve him, and she disappeared in the direction of the kitchen. He wondered whether this was how she treated all her customers.

She returned a few minutes later with a shabby wooden

tray on which was placed a bowl of kimchi and a kettle of wine.

'I need supper, too. Can you get me something to eat with the wine?' he enquired.

'Is this your first trip to the hamlet?' She responded to his request with a question, procrastinating in a manner most unusual for a proprietress of a tavern.

'No, but I might as well be a stranger. I wonder whether you can let me stay overnight.'

She ignored his request for a bed and remained silent, measuring him up.

'Is there any reason why I can't?' he pressed.

Only then did she consent reluctantly. 'Well, let me see. These days we seldom have travellers who stay overnight. We don't have any decent food, and you may not find the sleeping arrangements particularly comfortable. But if you don't mind roughing it I can't refuse.'

He replied that he did not mind at all. He tried to justify to himself her somewhat lukewarm reception, reasoning that the people of the southern provinces were scrupulous and had a simple pride in their business when rendering services for money, refusing to appear too solicitous. He found no reason to be upset.

'I guess things haven't improved much for the village, even though the inlet has been filled and turned into farms.' Drinking alone, the traveller talked to the woman as she worked in the kitchen just a few steps away, preparing supper for him. His remark triggered a friendlier response from her.

After a long interval she said, 'I wonder. Our business, this run-down roadside tavern, depends on the goodwill of the villagers, but it seems that people don't become any better-natured with the improvements in farming.' Holding a bucket of waste water in one hand, she stood amid the tangled wisps of smoke that arose from the fire of pine needles in the hearth. She searched her memory and ferreted out bits of information about the fortunes of the tavern in the past. 'I don't deny it,' she reflected somewhat wistfully, 'there was a time here, around ten years ago, I guess, when the labourers queued to be served. It was while the dam was under construction. But once the job was finished, so was business.'

'It must be because the crane cannot fly over Immortal Crane Village any more, I imagine,' the man mumbled, self-absorbed. Stirred by the woman's remark, which held a trace of grievance, he had become aware of the darkness creeping across the field in the direction of Gwaneumbong Mountain. He continued. 'I see that Immortal Crane Village exists now in name only. With no water in the inlet, the mountain has lost its reflection, and the crane can no longer take flight. So the crane village is without a crane, and, like the inlet, the people's hearts must have gone dry.'

At that moment there was a sound of the door of the inner room being pushed open, and a voice declared loudly, 'There is no reason why the crane can't fly, even with the water drained from the inlet.'

The proprietor must have been eavesdropping. He emerged carrying a lighted candle in his hand. Without uttering a greeting, he approached the traveller and continued enigmatically. 'For a while, after they blocked the seawater, we believed as you do. Without water how could the mountain show its reflection? But lately something has changed. You, my dear sir, may not be able to see it, but the crane has once again begun to fly over the dried-up inlet.'

The tavern-keeper seemed keenly interested in gauging the traveller's reaction and stared at his face. The traveller began to suspect that the proprietor was trying to prick his curiosity as he went on, 'A few years ago a woman came to this village. When she left the crane began to fly once more. I assume that you must have heard the story of the flying crane of this village.'

A sense of foreboding began to stir in the traveller's mind: the dead crane flies again after a woman's visit . . . He could feel that the proprietor, having already made an inroad to his thoughts, was trying to spark his curiosity. Tension gripped him as he looked at his host's face. Illuminated by the faint candle-light, he saw that the face was carved with the deep weariness of a man on the threshold of old age. Suddenly, in that face with its reddened high cheekbones and thick eyebrows, he discerned an image, the forgotten face of a boy beckoning from the dark recess of memory.

The traveller heard his heart beating louder, and he found himself lowering his voice, as was his habit in stressful situations. 'That's really the strangest thing I have ever heard, I won't deny it. I heard such a story long time ago: the story of the soaring crane. But who is the woman who passed through this village? Who is she whose visit caused the earthbound crane to soar once more?'

The traveller began to think that he had not come here in vain. The proprietor had allowed his expectations to grow. The guest encouraged his host to tell him the story of the woman and the crane, how she had caused it to fly again, but the host was not forthcoming. He hesitated and mumbled, 'I doubt it has anything to do with you, my honoured brother. But after your meal I may let you hear about it, just to pass the time.' The guest took this to mean that his host wanted to postpone telling the story. The proprietor moved away from his guest.

The traveller had read his host's mind. Although the

proprietor had not asked his guest why he was so anxious to hear the tale, the host seemed eager to disclose everything. Evidently he held his story back to increase his guest's sense of anticipation.

The traveller's intuition was right. Alone in the back room of the tavern he was restless, tormented by the disquieting presentiment he had felt earlier. Soon after his supper he went into the *maru*. He found that the proprietor had already returned to the same position as before and had the wine table brought in. The host sat with an empty wine cup in front of him, expecting his guest to join him. Without a word, and without a moment's hesitation, he filled the empty cup and raised it to his guest. The traveller took a seat facing his host. He, too, remained silent.

The field outside the tavern was illuminated by the full moon, and even without candlelight it was bright enough for the drinking companions.

The traveller drained the cup and handed it back to his host. The cup changed hands again. Then, even before being asked, the proprietor began his tale.

'Let me see. It was about thirty years ago. I was an errand boy in this tavern.' He began the story with his childhood recollection, paying little attention to chronology, an opening that was somewhat abrupt for the listener. And while the host's narrative was chaotic – cutting off the beginning and the end – the traveller's expression remained unmoved. He already had an intuition of what the speaker would say.

'One autumn day,' the proprietor continued, 'an extraordinary singing pair, a father and daughter, came to this tavern. The father's hair was half-white, and the daughter was barely nine years old. Both were renowned singers of the pansori of the southern region, and, as young as I was, I was aware that I was listening to exceptional songs.' The proprietor's voice deepened as he continued the story that he had locked away inside him like it was his most precious possession. The traveller listened without saying a word, focused and expectant. The host continued, ignoring the traveller's demeanour, which by now was betraying an inner struggle.

'It was mainly the father who sang. On rare occasions when he permitted the daughter to sing, he did so in order that she should learn. But those of us who listened to her agreed that her voice was just as deep and proud as his. Since their arrival the tavern was always full, for song-loving customers returned time and again. The songman would never leave the tavern to perform elsewhere, so the villagers had to come to the tavern to hear his songs, crossing the inlet. The father would sit here in this tavern, and when the tide filled the inlet and the mountain transformed itself into a crane the songman would begin to sing with the vision of the crane his only companion. When the father and daughter sang, accompanied by the soaring crane, there was no telling whether the immortal crane had invited the singers to sing or whether the songs had inspired the crane to fly. This went on for perhaps several months, and during that time I realized that the father had something else preoccupying him deep inside his mind. How shall I put it? It was not just because of the sight of the crane that he sang but more that his young daughter should engrave in her mind and singing the landscape of the inlet of the flying crane. At the end of those months he must have believed that what he had wanted had been accomplished. The daughter's singing had much improved, becoming more dignified, more solemn. And then, suddenly, they left the village. We have heard no word of them since then.'

His throat becoming tight, the proprietor paused to drink

some more wine. After emptying the cup, he handed it to his guest, which the traveller accepted without a word. It was by this gesture that he urged the host on. The story continued.

'After the singers had left, with no promise of return, many of the villagers were unable to forget their songs. Many more wished that they would some day return. At any event, for many years the villagers talked about the two singers and their songs, but the pair never returned. Eventually the memory of the father and daughter began to fade from the villagers' minds. After the inlet had become a field and Gwaneumbong Mountain lost its reflection the tale of the pansori singers was largely forgotten. I believe it was in the spring, about two years ago, when the inlet had already been filled for seven or eight years, that the woman returned one day out of nowhere.'

The host paused to examine his guest. The story was reaching its climax. When the wine cup was pushed over to his side of the table the traveller drank the contents down in a single gulp. Finding it increasingly difficult to suppress his anticipation, as he handed the cup back he asked his host, 'Did you say a woman? You mean the daughter of the song-man?'

'Who else?' The proprietor chided the guest lightly for his interjection but continued, 'She had grown older. Or, rather, her songs reflected the passage of time. And her father, her teacher, had been dead for many years. But I recognized her straight away, and she also knew immediately who I was.'

'What was her reason for returning to the village?' the guest once more interrupted.

But this time, the host did not show any inclination to reproach his guest. 'I suppose she must have wished to see the flying crane of her childhood. But she came with more important business to settle.' The tavern-keeper was impatient to continue his narrative, and after this response was about to carry on.

But the traveller interrupted the man one more time. 'Business? What business?' He needed to participate in the other's recounting of the tale in order to appease his own growing apprehension.

The proprietor ignored his guest's question. His voice now suggested that he would not broach any more interruptions from the listener. He pronounced each word in a weighty yet urgent tone, implying that the revelation he was about to make was the very thing he had been guarding as a secret so carefully for years and that the time had come at last to tell the tale.

It had been late evening when the daughter arrived at the tavern. This time she was not with her father but with a man of late middle age, carrying a drum and a fine-looking wooden box on his back. The box was revealed to be a small casket containing the bones of her deceased father, who had died somewhere near the town of Boseong some twenty years earlier. The daughter had gone there and exhumed the bones from the grave and returned with them to have a new burial in Immortal Crane Village. The villagers speculated that it was her father's last request to be buried at the foothill of the mountain and that the daughter's long-cherished desire had been to fulfil that wish. Since the village had been renowned for having the most propitious burial grounds, there was not a single plot available in all the land near the mountain. Those plots that remained had already been claimed. Unless she resorted to stealing a site or to embarking on a secret burial in someone else's plot, the daughter knew it would be difficult to accomplish her mission. There were very few people in the village who still remembered her songs and the soaring crane. Those who had heard the story about her and her father suddenly became watchful and pretended to busy themselves in the maintenance of their own burial plots.

The daughter was not in a hurry. She never betrayed her impatience; she simply spent her days singing, so that when the setting sun's gossamer rays enveloped the village her song would resonate in the gathering darkness around the tavern:

'Hampyeong heaven and earth, this old man . . .'

The woman sang in a voice mellowed with age, and her male companion accompanied her on his drum. Her songs gradually drew the villagers to the tavern again, and as the days passed her songs tore at her listeners' hearts.

Her singing continued for a few more days, and in the meantime a peculiar change was taking place in the community. No villager had offered her a burial plot, but as they listened to the daughter's songs each understood that sooner or later the father would find a place to be buried in their midst. They all came to know that this would be the most natural thing in the world, yet how and where they had no idea. But, listening to her songs, the villagers indulged in their vague speculation that it would happen somehow.

The proprietor, more than anyone else from the village, perceived that there was a hidden meaning in the woman's songs and understood what it was. He had only to wait for the time of its revelation. And one day such a time came:

'Hair dishevelled like arrowroot stalks,
In a prison room sat a solitary apparition.'

The woman sang with singular effort that day. Only at the midnight did she finish, and only then did the villagers cross the fields to their homes to sleep. After they had all departed, the woman, too, left the tavern and disappeared into the darkness of the night, her companion leading the way. Strapped on his back was the wooden box containing her father's bones. That night she engaged in a secret burial somewhere and then was gone. She never again returned to the tavern.

'Then, after she left, the attitude of the villagers inexplicably changed.' The story was coming to an end. 'She disappeared overnight, but the villagers asked one another no questions. They seemed to have known that sooner or later she would leave them in such a manner and could even guess the reason for her sudden departure, yet they never said a word. I suppose they had tacitly agreed that it was for the best. Two years have passed since she left, and even now no one knows where she buried the bones. There might be some who do, but they don't speak of it.' The tavern-keeper stopped and began to study the traveller's reaction.

His guest remained silent. Neither spoke at this point. The sound of the wind whistling through the pine groves had abated. The proprietor, however, appeared not to have quite finished his story. Noting that the kettle of wine was now empty, he stood up from his seat with it and disappeared into the kitchen. He returned with a fresh supply, poured some into the cups and steadily observed the traveller's expression.

The host cast a determined look at his guest, challenging him to speak. But the traveller's silence was obdurate; his lips were closed tightly in an effort to stem the tide of premonition from which he could no longer escape. Even more unbearable to him, however, was his host's silence. There was no contest; the tavern-keeper had won.

'Wasn't the woman blind?' the traveller blurted out, defeated by the silence. He was convinced of the accuracy of his speculation and had the answer already. He did not need the host's reply.

As if he had been telling the long tale only to elicit this question, the proprietor hastily answered, 'Ah, it was indeed so. But did I forget to tell you that earlier? She was blind, yes. Her elderly companion led her everywhere.'

But still the tone of the tavern-keeper suggested that there was something more that he was not yet quite ready to divulge. He did not ask his guest how he had known that the woman was blind. Just as the host seemed to have read the guest's intentions and thoughts, so the traveller remained undisturbed by the host's feigned ignorance. Words had become irrelevant between them; their silence betrayed their thoughts.

It was once more the traveller who spoke first. He lamented, 'No use. It's no use. What good does it do, now that Immortal Crane Village is without the flying crane? She buried her father's remains in vain.' His words sank inwards, and he fell quiet.

However, these words seemed to have been all that was necessary to satisfy the host. Up till then the stranger had not revealed his relationship to the woman, but the host had observed the man's anxious expression when he was told about the blind woman who had come to Immortal Crane Village without the crane to bury her father's ashes. It was at this point that the host noted the pain on his guest's face. This was enough for the tavern-keeper; everything was clear.

The proprietor spoke again. 'But I wonder if you have forgotten what I told you earlier, my dear sir. It was not for nothing that she did what she did. Because, you see, after she left the crane once again began to soar. She made it possible for the crane to fly in Immortal Crane Village. Who saw the crane that took flight from the dry inlet of this village? It was this blind woman.'

The host was ready to launch into the story of how the crane came to fly again in the village, how the blind woman saw it before anyone else. Once he began he paid no attention to the guest's reaction. It was not the tavern-keeper's concern how the traveller would interpret his tale or whether or not he would even believe this strange mythic story, because he himself was convinced by its veracity. He was determined to tell his guest everything – all that he had kept locked deep in his heart.

Tight-lipped, the traveller strained his ears to catch the tale of his host, the story of the woman who had become the crane in her songs.

'Don't go, O, don't go,
Maiden Sim. Don't go.'

She had spent days just singing. After listening to her for a few days the proprietor realized that it was only when the tide should have been filling the inlet that she would sing, and she would do this only after seating herself on the tavern's *maru* and while casting her eyes over the inlet water like a person who can see.

One day, when the proprietor had returned from the village at sunset, the woman and her companion were preparing to sing seated on the *maru*. Afraid to disturb her concentration, he walked in silently and paused for a while behind the gate to observe the two.

She did not start singing immediately, and the tavern-keeper began to listen in to a strange conversation between them. As he listened, he was overcome by a peculiar sensation. It was mostly the woman who asked the questions, and her elderly companion simply listened and gave short responses.

'Today is the second of the month, isn't it?' she asked, awaiting the reply with total concentration.

'Perhaps,' the companion said abstractedly, looking at her.

'The inlet is being filled. I hear the sound of the water coming in,' she said, addressing no one in particular and moving her head gently. She gathered her attention to listen, as though she could actually hear the sound of the sea beyond the dam some distance from the tavern.

The proprietor reckoned that it was indeed almost high tide. Prior to the construction of the dam the inlet would have been filled with seawater by then. But the water had been blocked off, and the inlet had disappeared long ago. However, the woman could still hear the tide rising, and she was urging her companion to listen as well, as he, with his eyes closed, allowed the sound of water reach to his ears.

She went on, 'Do you hear that? I mean the sound of the rushing water, dear sir?'

'Yes, indeed, I seem to hear it.' His answer was soothing and his voice gentle, comforting her.

The proprietor was completely taken aback by the woman's next remark.

'If you hear the sound of the tide, then surely you must see the crane flying over the water, too.' And she described to her companion the panorama that was inscribed in her mind. 'Do you see it, sir? When the water filled the inlet Gwaneumbong Mountain descended on the water's surface in the shape of a crane and soared to the sky. Now, do you see it?'

'Yes, I do see it now. I see the water, the inlet and the mountain beyond. I clearly see the crane taking flight.' The man allowed his eyes and ears to submit to the woman's will.

Her empty eyes surveyed the terrain before her, chasing the movement of the soaring crane. The woman spun about to face her companion, who was almost ready to begin the singing, and lamented, 'Long ago, at about this time, my father's songs and the crane strolled together over the water.'

Listening to their conversation the proprietor was mystified. There was no longer water or a mountain reflection. Perhaps it was because of her blindness that she could detect the water and the crane, which those with eyes that could see had missed. Clear sight could behold only a parched land, which could not mirror the mountain's reflection. Her sightlessness, he fantasized, gave her the ability to see the vanished water and the invisible mountain reflection. And gradually these fantastic thoughts he had entertained turned into a mystical faith for him.

> 'Boundless Yellow Sea, the waves' roar.
> Seagulls of Baekbinju fly into Hongyo.'

The woman began to sing at last. In her voice, surging from the depths of her soul, vibrating through her viscera, the proprietor, too, began to see. Leaning against the gatepost and with his eyes closed, he listened, and as he listened he could see the long-forgotten crane slowly unfurling its wings and taking flight. As the woman's long, lingering songs continued, they brought back the tide water: it began to rush into the inlet of Immortal Crane Village, and with it the sacred crane surfaced and circled over the water.

From that day on the proprietor believed in the woman's crane. Every day, at what would have been high tide, she sang, and her songs would bring the water flooding back into the inlet and cause the crane to fly serenely.

Then, one day, suddenly she was gone. Yet even after the woman had left the village the proprietor continued to hear her songs just as before, and at such times her songs transformed the land into the inlet, and her songs and the crane lingered over the water. Finally she herself had metamorphosed into the crane.

'No, I don't think she has left the village,' the proprietor would tell the people. 'She became the crane and circles this village for ever, high up in the sky.'

His immediate neighbours and the villagers did not dismiss his remarks as hallucination, perhaps because they, too, missed the woman who had left them so abruptly. Just as they closed their eyes when she had buried her father's bones somewhere in secret, they would not question the reasons for her hasty departure or her destination. And even when the tavern-keeper rambled on with his preposterous tales, the villagers put up with him, their solemn expressions perhaps betraying their desire to share in his belief.

Affected by the host's story, the traveller was visibly on the verge of exhaustion. He showed no interest in the wine cup, which he let his hand reach over and pick up from time to time.

The storyteller, too, looked just as worn out. In baring his heart to his guest, he was a man who had accomplished his life's task. What his guest would say in response to his tale was a matter of no importance. Once in a while the wind would rise from the hills behind the tavern, rustle through pine branches, reach them and then whistle past their ears as it raced towards the sea. The sounds of the wind and the sea beyond the dam fused into one.

It was once more the traveller who broke the stillness, unable to bear the silence. 'I appreciate you telling me the story,' he began. His low voice was now composed, implying that he had nothing more to hide from his host. 'But you failed to mention another person in your story.'

The tavern-keeper looked steadily across the table at the traveller, who sat bathed in the moonlight.

The guest continued, 'I am talking about the time when the father and daughter came to this village when you were a boy. I believe there was a brother who accompanied her songs on the drum. But you intentionally omitted him from your account.' He looked straight into his host's face.

'Yes, indeed,' the proprietor nodded emphatically, a gesture indicating that he, too, had nothing more to hide from his guest. 'I also know that the brother had run away from his father and his defenceless baby sister. She told me everything.'

'Then you must also know that the brother and the sister do not share the father's blood and are thus practically unrelated. And you must know why the young brother left them. She must have told you that it was because he could not carry out his scheme to murder his stepfather, against whom he harboured a grudge.'

The host nodded again. His head moved ponderously.

His guest persisted. 'Then, why didn't you mention the brother?'

'It was because I had an impression that you might be someone who knows the brother. I suspected it the moment you first mentioned the soaring crane.'

'Then why did you neglect to tell me about him until now? Was it your intention to deceive me to the end?'

'No, that was never my intention. On the contrary, for the past two years I have been waiting for the man, her brother. I have been telling myself that when I meet him I will tell him all I know. I believed I had an obligation. Only by telling him everything would I feel I had done right thing.'

'So you mean to say that you knew all along that one day her brother would come here?'

'She told me so. She told me that her brother might come here looking for her. I was sure she really believed it.'

'Why didn't you tell me so right from the start?'

'It was because she told me not to. She made me promise that when her brother came to me looking for her never to open my mouth before the brother asks first, even if I see him suffer, unable to overcome the pain of bitterness. So that's the reason why I have been observing you and waiting for you to make your confession.' The proprietor stopped and scrutinized his guest's expression.

Once again, the traveller's lips were closed tightly. As he gazed down at the moon's reflection on the inner courtyard a flash of remorse crossed his face.

The host went on, his voice slowly stirring his guest's pain-ridden soul. 'I wonder whether she really meant it when she made me promise not to tell anything to her brother before he asks. She must have already known that he would come and that he would somehow hear the story. She left only after extracting from me one key promise. She asked me to tell her brother not to go on looking for her. Do you remember what I said earlier? I told you that she had become the crane, and even now she is flying over the inlet. I didn't make that up. These are the words she said: "Tell my brother not to go on looking for me, that I will remain here as the crane, for ever flying over the sky of Immortal Crane Village." That was her last request. True to her words, she faded away that night, taking the form of a crane and ascending to the sky.'

The following morning after breakfast the traveller was putting on his shoes after having exchanged words of farewell with the proprietor's wife when the tavern-keeper said to him, 'Before you leave, don't you wish to visit the grave of the songman and pay your respects to his soul?' The host felt his guest's probing gaze, questioning his motive in enquiring. He added hurriedly, 'Of course, it's none of my concern. What I meant was that if you do wish to do so I can show you the way.'

Only then did the traveller let a faint meaningful smile appear on his face. 'I knew it all along. It was a task beyond the ability of a blind woman and a man advanced in age. Someone must have helped them to bury the bones.' He shook his head. 'It's no use now. The songman is buried with the *han* of his own making during his life on earth. What's the use now that he is no longer of this world? I'd rather leave this way.' With these words the traveller turned around, stepped into the freshly swept yard and began to walk away.

The proprietor did not press him further. He silently followed the traveller through the brush gate, but he hesitated for a moment, unwilling to let his guest go, implying that there were still unspoken words. 'So, did the brother see his half-sister after he ran away from the songman, or was that the last time?' The tavern-keeper's question came abruptly.

'Yes. He saw her once after that. It was about three years ago in a tavern near Jangheung.' The traveller walked on, and his words lingered, sounding like he was talking about someone else. 'But, right to the end, the brother could not tell the blind woman that he was her half-brother. And when he went back there again to look for her, she had already left, leaving no trace.'

The proprietor trailed after the traveller idly, and the guest did not discourage his host from sharing his steps in a final farewell. The morning sun of late autumn was uncommonly crystalline and the whistling of the wind through the pine groves especially pleasant. They were now entering the path though the woods, and all at once the field and Gwaneumbong Mountain came into view. Only then did the traveller pause. He waited for his host's last words before he turned the bend in the hill.

'So,' the tavern-keeper asked finally, intuiting the meaning of the traveller's silence. 'Do you still intend to go on looking for your half-sister?'

'No.' The traveller shook his head, intending to put the other man's mind at ease. 'What's the use now? To tell you the truth, I did not really come here to look for her. I was just hoping for a chance to hear the epilogue to her story. Some day, if I desire, I wonder whether I might come back here again. I might wish to revisit the Immortal Crane Village just to listen to the wandering songs of the woman whose soul has transmigrated into that of the crane.' He listened to try to catch the songs, which floated out from somewhere in the village. His eyes became hazy, as if he were gazing into a mirage that had appeared riding on the song's refrain, the vision of the woman soaring in the sky in the shape of the crane. The wind whistled once again and receded beyond the hill.

The host stopped and turned back as the traveller reached the hilly path in the pine groves. By the time he arrived at the gate of the tavern the other was about to climb the hill. The proprietor waited for his guest to reach the top of it and move on. But the traveller did not move. At lunch time he was still crouching on the same spot. Towards the end of the day the proprietor gave up and stopped watching him from a distance. The traveller remained there all day. It was not until the sun had almost set that he finally disappeared from the hilltop.

The proprietor had waited most of the day for the man to move on, occupying himself by mending the inn gate. When he looked up once more, expecting the traveller to be in the same spot, his figure had disappeared and in its place just blue sky. Suddenly the tavern-keeper felt a lacerating sense of desolation. During the day, while the traveller sat on the hill-top, the proprietor had imagined that he could hear a voice ringing out from the direction of the hill. It sounded to him like the woman's voice from long ago or perhaps that of the traveller. But the sound had ceased with the man's departure. He could not tell whether he was dreaming. He could not, despite his efforts, determine whether or not he had actually heard singing. But, it didn't matter much any more. He was reluctant to know the truth. He saw no reason to separate fact from imagination. Through the haze of his mind he saw one more peculiar sight. He looked up to gaze upon the hilltop where the traveller had been. There was a snow-white crane unfurling its wings, taking flight and circling the deep-blue sky.

BIRD AND TREE

A MAN STOOD among the trees in his yard, pausing to rest after covering them with straw sheaths to ready them for winter. As he stood gazing at the sky for a long time, it was hard to distinguish his form from that of the trees around him.

The traveller was on the road again after having journeyed to Boseong, Jangheung and Gangjin, mostly on foot. From the outset he had had no interest in making a trip that required any kind of vehicle. During the previous three weeks he had wandered at a leisurely pace, looking like someone without a care in the world. He experienced many encounters along the way, some in the folds of mountains and others along the roads edged by seashores with their sparkling waves. Those were the memories of landscapes that no one in a car could have captured. He treasured what he absorbed through every pore of his being at each pause in his journey: the drift of the wind in the pines, the scent of the sea. He was afraid that if he ensconced himself in a vehicle his travel-worn body would relax and the grains of memory that had collected in his clothing would dissipate like dust in the wind as his fatigue eased.

Now he reached the point where he could not bear to walk on any further. He had just left Gangjin, and as he was entering the Haenam region he found himself wanting a place to rest overnight.

A new village promised a new day, a new setting. No need to hurry. The last blink of the setting sun, now as small as a deer's tail, rushed in the late autumn's waning dusk.

The traveller was making his way towards a town, only a cigarette smoke away, but he dragged his feet, fighting an impulse to collapse on the roadside and take some rest. Finally, as he reached the edge of town, he noticed a grove, apparently an orchard, and the incongruous figure of a man standing still among the trees.

The orchard nestled at the foot of one of the mountain ridges that bordered the town like a screen to the north. The saplings had been planted randomly. Among the persimmon, citron and pomegranate trees that the local people in the southern provinces grew for their families to enjoy each season there were also commercially valuable fruit trees such as pear, walnut and peach. Then there were some tall pines and camellias standing alongside the other trees and shrubs; these must have been there before the orchard had come into existence, their long branches outstretched in strange patterns. In the chill of late autumn the grove, with its chaotically planted trees, the leaves of which were now half fallen, conveyed an impression of abandonment.

It was this that lured the traveller to the orchard, and before realizing it he had changed his course, so that instead of heading towards the town he approached the grove instead. It might have been the thatched dwelling he had glimpsed among the trees that awakened in him a long-forgotten dream. He found a singular solace and respite in the landscape of decay.

As he neared the entrance to the orchard he stopped at the makeshift gate and moved closer to the man he had spotted. He had just finished covering a citron tree to protect it against the harsh winter wind and was continuing the process with other trees, stopping to rest periodically. The wide leaves on the persimmon trees had turned dark brown, and most of them had fallen and scattered on the ground. The traveller observed the figure of the man etched against the landscape. Dressed in work clothes, supporting his back with a hand, he stood quietly looking up at a treetop. One could not distinguish his figure from the trees around him. It was as if he was one of them.

The traveller lost track of his destination and stood transfixed, watching the man. Becoming aware of the presence of another, the farmer slowly turned to face him. Then, suddenly and inexplicably, he lifted his hand and beckoned.

At first the traveller thought he was imagining things. He spun around to see whether there was someone behind him, but there was no one. As he stood there, perplexed, the man once again waved to him, an unmistakable gesture inviting him to enter the orchard. There was no way he could remain where he was and ignore the summons, nor could he turn to leave, pretending he had not seen the gesture. He felt as though he was under a spell, but he followed the path into the grove. Once inside he saw that there was a rich variety of trees. The young fruit trees being prepared for winter stood packed closely among more mature ones. Some were still in leaf, others already covered with straw sheaths. In addition to the fruit trees were many seedlings apparently being cultivated as ornamental house plants. Tropical plants such as palm trees and cactus grew like weeds in the yard beyond the orchard. Rocks lay everywhere, some along the path, others along the edge of the grove. They were of fine quality, good enough for rockeries, and the collectors of unusual and precious boulders and large stones would no doubt have paid handsomely for them, perhaps enough to sell them on commercially. But they were numerous and obviously too little regarded to be of interest to the man in the orchard and merely added a further air of desolation to its already neglected appearance.

By the time the traveller had approached the man he had returned to his work on the trees, protecting a citron by wrapping each of its branches with a wad of straw sheath. He gave no word of greeting. He was so preoccupied with what he was doing and apparently unaware of the traveller who stood behind him that he appeared to have totally forgotten his earlier invitation.

The traveller waited a while for the man to interrupt his work. He felt at ease with this individual who paid him so little attention, just as the bleak landscape had given him an exquisite sensation of familiarity.

However, the traveller soon discovered that the farmer was not unaware of his presence and had not forgotten about him. He was simply confident that the other would continue standing there, waiting.

Shortly after the man grew tired. He put his hand on his waist, stretched languidly and gazed at the sky. Seizing the moment, the traveller ventured to speak to him. 'You have so many trees here. Good trees for a fine orchard, I would say.'

Only then did the man acknowledge the traveller's presence and respond quite casually, as if talking to a neighbour who had come to watch him work. 'I doubt it. They are nothing but worthless shrubs, barely good enough for flying creatures to roost in.'

The traveller was perplexed by the man's words and the general way in which he behaved. He wondered if his arrival had been expected, precisely at this time, at dusk, the farmer ready to usher his twilight visitor into his house as a guest. The man shook the dirt and shreds of straw from his hands and emerged from the orchard to lead the way, as if he had intended to do this all along. All the while he pretended to ignore the traveller, uttering no word of invitation nor making any remark.

He began to walk casually towards the thatched house a few steps ahead of his companion.

The traveller paused for a moment, unable to make up his mind whether to follow where he was being led. The farmer turned his head and urged him on as he hesitated.

'Why are you standing there like that? Let us go into the house.' He seemed surprised by the traveller's indecision, and what he said were unmistakably words of welcome to his guest. When the traveller still did not move the farmer urged him once more, this time with greater encouragement. 'You are a guest who would honour me by entering my house at the end of the day, and I cannot let you leave. So, please, let's go inside. I know that if you go into town you will get a room at an inn, but since you're already inside my gate and the day is almost over I urge you to spend the night with me, although you might find the accommodation less comfortable.'

The way the man spoke, almost in a commanding tone, caused the traveller to wonder whether he had some ulterior motive or whether he simply represented that rarity, one of those genuinely good-natured country folk who took pleasure in inviting a stranger into their homes.

The traveller found himself feeling even more perplexed at his own growing sense of calm as he trailed behind his host. Rows of persimmon and fig trees, almost bare of their leaves, encircled the inner yard of the farmer's humble thatched house. A barn and a tool-shed stood at the back. When they reached the house the man sat on the *maru* and, rubbing his hands vigorously to remove some the dirt that caked them, called inside, 'Where are you? Are you there?'

The man's wife came into view, rounding the corner of the house, having just emerged from the barn. At the point of interruption by her husband she must have been feeding pigs, for she carried a gourd with water still dripping from it. She wore a white towel on her head, and her weary weather-beaten face – the face of a farmer's wife – looked almost ten years older than that of her husband.

No sooner did she approach than the farmer said abruptly, 'We have a guest. I want you to prepare a wine table for us.' The traveller did not have a chance to decline the offer. There was no awkwardness in the farmer's request to his wife; he was doing only what he was expected to do. His wife also appeared unruffled. Although the husband offered no explanation, she displayed no curiosity about the reason for the guest's visit or the manner of his appearance. Neither did she show the slightest resentment towards this stranger who had dropped in unexpectedly, imposing himself at this late stage in the day.

'I have nothing ready. So it may take some time,' she said matter-of-factly and moved in the direction of the kitchen. But she did not make the men wait long. She was as prompt as the proprietress of a tavern would have been, whose business it was to serve her customers without delay. Even before the traveller could express his gratitude she had returned carrying a small table with simple fare: some vegetable dishes and a bottle of wine. She showed no sign of embarrassment in presenting such a modest table, just as she had betrayed no resentment at the unexpected guest.

'In this rural household of ours, this is all I can offer for now. Do have some wine with these dishes,' she said simply, pushing the table towards them.

'We need a couple of carp from the pond for our guest. We haven't had company for such a long time,' the husband said to his wife, sounding somewhat irritable. And as she prepared to withdraw, he added, 'Be sure to tell Jeong-bae when he comes home to put some fire in the room across from the *maru*. Our guest will stay there tonight. Tell Jeong-bae to sleep somewhere else in town tonight.'

'Very well,' she responded and returned to the kitchen.

Watching his spouse disappear carrying a bamboo basket with a net heaped in it, the host opened the bottle and invited the traveller to drink. 'Right now, let's wet our throats with this.'

The behaviour of man and wife was inscrutable to him, but somehow the traveller ended up as a genuine guest in the household. Cups were exchanged between the guest and the host. Seated on the *maru*, the traveller listened to the host talk about his life. All the while he remained unable to fathom either the innermost thoughts of his host or the source of his goodwill. He displayed no intention of revealing why he had invited the traveller into his home, nor did he show any interest in learning anything about the stranger. The traveller had no choice but to wait for the host to volunteer this information.

The host's conversation circled around mundane subjects such as his orchard, the household chores and so on, without touching on more important matters. Seemingly uninterested in the traveller's background, he chatted freely about his daily life. He and his wife had an unmarried son, Jeong-bae. They farmed for a living, and from the way he spoke it became clear that the large orchard and woods that surrounded the house contributed little to their household income. As he listened to his host, the traveller realized the farmer had a peculiar attitude towards his trees.

'I enjoy growing fruit trees, just as I enjoy cultivating flowers and plants. When they bear fruit we share them with our neighbours, and occasionally, if we have more than enough for our own use, I take some to market to sell. You can't make a living by watching flowers bloom and plants grow, can you?' This was the answer the man gave when the traveller enquired why they bothered to struggle with farming when there were just three of them.

If they improved the orchard and increased its productivity and raised domestic animals, the traveller suggested, the income could provide for the family comfortably. The man seemed indifferent to the possibilities of gainfully profiting from his fruit trees. While they sat there the traveller observed a variety of fine plants dotted throughout the yard which might fetch a considerable sum of money if sold to city dwellers as garden plants or *bonsai*. He asked his host whether he might be interested in opening a nursery garden.

The man's answer was somewhat peremptory. 'I've never thought about it. I just cultivate plants for the love of it. I understand that there are people who do such things for money, but I prefer to share my plants for nothing.' He was implying that such worldly considerations were despicable; flowers were for appreciation, not for material gain. All he did was to plant and nurture his trees and plants so that the trees would bear fruit and the flowering plants bloom. He helped them to grow with beauty. He had no thought of depending on them for his livelihood.

The traveller now understood why the orchard had the strange lack of order and mysterious appeal of a neglected plot. He wondered if the farmer's dependence only on his small piece of land for subsistence reflected a lack of awareness of the prevailing materialist culture. Alternatively, it could be that he was one of those rare stubborn individuals of rigid morality who intentionally turn their backs on money-making ventures. When the trees bore fruit he took it to market, but he never thought of selling his trees to provide ornamental garden displays for urban households in order to top up his income. For the family's subsistence he relied purely on his small farm, which exemplified his attitude of self-sufficiency and his contempt for the market mentality.

This impression was confirmed when the son returned home from the fields. He showed up when his father and the guest had already finished two bottles of wine. He carried a shovel on his shoulder and a bamboo basket of live carp, each the size of a hand, snapping and jumping in their cage. His mother followed. The son must have helped her catch the fish in their pond on his way home.

'I just wanted a few slices of raw meat for sashimi and the rest of the fish for soup. Why so many? Don't let the brood stock dwindle in the pond.'

'I need what you can't use, Father,' the son replied as he put the basket down on the stepping stone to the *maru*, unruffled by his father's admonishment.

'What do you mean, you need fish, too? Are you off for a drink tonight?'

'We did community roadwork today, so the neighbours are getting together tonight to drink. They want me to bring something along to eat.'

'Of course, I know that a hard day's work is an occasion for drinking, but if they want fish from my pond you tell them to stock it with a fresh supply of fry once in a while.' The man's remarks didn't sound to the traveller as if he were chiding his son for drinking or wasting his fish. The father changed the subject. 'So the work is almost complete?'

'Not yet. We need a couple of more days to get it ready for the cultivator. We have a lot more work to do.'

'Well, if you have work to do tomorrow, don't stay up late and get too drunk,' the father warned.

'I won't,' the son replied, picking up the basket. 'I'm leaving now. I'll sleep in town tonight since you have a guest.'

'You haven't had dinner yet, and you're heading off for drinking party?'

The son was not going to accept discipline from his father and, not hiding his desire to get going, answered quickly, 'I'll have a bite to eat when I get there.'

'All right. I understand. But before you go prepare the fish and put some firewood in your room.'

'Don't worry. I won't leave before I've done my chores.'

The young man turned and walked off towards the kitchen without showing any interest in the guest. The father did not insist on proper manners from his son, just as he had been indifferent to his wife's demeanour.

'That's my son,' the man said to the traveller, almost as an afterthought and only after the young man had already disappeared.

The traveller found himself warmed by the spontaneous intimacy of the father and son. The simple words they had exchanged about the gathering of the neighbours for a drink after their communal labour reminded him of the family elders' conversations when they used to assemble on the night of ancestor-worship holiday. The exchange between father and son revived good memories. Their self-sufficient life engendered freedom and love of mankind. He felt the goodness of the human heart arising from the interaction between the family members, like evening smoke billowing out of a thatched farmhouse, enveloping him in its warmth. The traveller finally understood what enabled such farmers to withstand isolation and enjoy a life of independence. But he was unwilling to convey his feelings to his host, for what he was experiencing was too elusive and precious for words.

'He seems to be a very trustworthy young man. Has he finished his schooling?' the traveller asked out of politeness, but he was also puzzled. The youth needed to be nurtured and disciplined, to become healthy in body and upright in mind. Moreover, it was only natural for those who had been deprived of education themselves, as the father obviously had been, to wish for their offspring a better future. The young man did not appear to have had much of an education, however. The traveller thought that the father must have had a reason for not ensuring a good education for his son, in spite of his seemingly comfortable circumstances.

'Did you say school?' The man's reply was what the traveller had expected; he insisted on doing everything his own way, even when it came to educating his son. 'He finished ninth grade at the local school,' the farmer volunteered and added, sounding apologetic, 'You have to send your children to high schools in Gwangju or other large towns, but my son refused to continue, and there was nothing I could do about it.'

The father had ensured that his reluctant son had gone to high school in Gwangju, but in less than two years the boy had returned home for good, saying he wanted to stay in his parents' house and farm. After his homecoming he worked obsessively on the farm like a man possessed by the rice-paddy ghost. The son had given up on education of his own accord, the father insisted. 'You cannot force a high official position on a reluctant candidate. Perhaps it's just as well. Getting an education in a city means acquiring the skills to compete with rivals and learn the means to relieve people of their money. Had he finished a few more years of city education I am sure he would have learned that sort of oneupmanship. But those who do not have the ambition to get ahead and to steal don't need to acquire such knowledge. Ninth grade is a sufficient level of education for my son to live comfortably among his neighbours, tilling his own land. He doesn't need to worry about being cheated or having his property stolen. There is nothing more he needs to learn. He knows the limits of his abilities and lives accordingly, keeping within his own province. In this respect, he deserves a lot of credit.'

The man had become talkative with drink. He defended the way he had brought his son up and his view of schooling. He maintained that a city education was nothing more than a way to teach pupils to satisfy their selfishness and greed. A better education, he suggested, was to leave a child to grow according to his own native ability rather than let the child's heart and mind be contaminated by a corrupt educational system. What he advocated was a far more profound educational theory. City folk might consider his view naive or incompatible with the modern world and dismiss it with a condescending smile as escapist and self-deluding, but the farmer's stubborn adherence to his views on education was something city-dwellers would be unable to comprehend, their ignorance stemming from a misunderstanding of human nature.

The traveller wondered if his host was aware that his own views on education were not widely shared and if his son had returned from his city high school because he realized his father's view on education was right. He was unable to reach any conclusion. Nevertheless, the traveller was convinced that the farmer's rejection of materialism, his understanding of his life's circumstances and his desire to live within its bounds must be the source of his generosity in inviting a stranger into his house. The traveller realized how much he had been affected by city life, how he had become petty, unable to accept an event at face value because he felt compelled to look for a hidden meaning. Still he questioned the host's motives: was it purely from the goodness of his heart that he had invited a stranger into his house, or were there other reasons for his hospitality?

He could find no answer, as he recalled the image of the man standing solidly among the trees and quietly beckoning to him.

By remaining silent the host gave the impression he knew everything about the traveller and that his guest understood why he had been invited into the house and offered a place to sleep. The visitor felt awkward questioning his host further, as supper was about to be served.

Host and guest moved into the inner room of the house. They sat facing one another with the dinner table between them. But before touching the food they resumed their drinking, first removing the rice bowls from the table and placing them beneath.

As the traveller scrutinized the table with its impeccably and painstakingly presented dishes, the questions he had puzzled over earlier once more rose in his mind.

He was amazed by the care with which the meal had been prepared. There were many kinds of vegetables on the table, all of them gathered from the garden and beautifully cooked. There was also a dish of freshly killed chicken; the wife must have killed it herself. In addition to the sashimi dish garnished with watercress, what was left of the fish after they had been filleted for the sashimi had been used to add substance and flavour to the radish soup. He had become an honoured guest indeed.

'I really don't deserve all this. I would have been happy just with wine. But this – it's too much!' Feeling uncomfortable and unable to know what else he could do to express his gratitude, the traveller continued to thank his host for the peculiar kindness that had been extended to him. Then, unable to contain his curiosity any longer, he questioned the farmer in order to try to fathom his motives. He started by saying, half in gratitude and half in compliment for the host's generosity, 'I suppose, respected host, that you truly enjoy having company, is that right?'

The host might have sensed something significant in his guest's probing, so while pouring out the wine he paused and looked straight into the face of his guest across the table, saying, 'Well, I do rather like company. But I must say I rarely entertain a guest. I think I made a mistake in this case. When I first saw you, I mistook you for someone else. It was an illusion I saw.' The host had been reluctant to divulge his motive for inviting the man into his house, now saying that what he had done had been in error.

This was not quite what the traveller had expected. It was now the guest who was in the dark. Only later was he to grasp what the farmer was saying.

'What do you mean you made a mistake?' The traveller had not anticipated that his host would be so candid – they had not even exchanged names. He wondered if the farmer had been waiting for his guest to ask the reason for the invitation.

'Did you know, my dear sir, that there are birds called "rainbirds" that sing only when it rains? Have you ever seen one of them?' the man asked as he handed the empty wine cup back to his guest after drinking from it first.

At this unexpected question the traveller hesitated for a moment, unable to grasp either the meaning of the query or his host's motive in asking it.

The man did not wait for a reply and went on, 'I had an elder brother. I don't remember having ever seen him when I was a child. It was only from others talking about him that I knew about him.' Now the subject had jumped from rainbirds to a brother who had left home.

The year his brother graduated from the town primary school an unusually large number of his schoolmates went to the neighbouring city of Mokpo for a high-school education. He had probably wished to go, too, but because of his family's circumstances had not even considered the possibility.

After most of his friends had left the town his brother had spent the entire spring doing nothing but flying kites in a barley field. One day the string tied to his kite broke, and the kite disappeared into the sky. Like the kite, he left home – apparently to seek his fortune in the city.

'I was too young to remember his leaving home. Many, many years later I heard my mother occasionally talk about it. That's how I know.'

After this aside the man went back to talking about the rain-bird, and the story of the bird was none other than the story of his brother. When he was growing up there was a bird that sang only on rainy days from spring through autumn. From the chestnut woods beyond the field, shrouded in the milky mist of summer rain, or from the dank pine groves on the hill, drenched in autumnal rain, the bird's mournful song floated out, at times from afar and at others near by.

'Poor thing, it can't find shelter from the cold rain,' he said to his mother.

She explained that it was a type of bird without a nest, so that when the weather was bad it had to search, crying out, looking for places to rest its rain-soaked body. When they heard the bird's cry the boy noticed that his mother's face would cloud over with anxiety. On some summer nights, black as lacquer, they would hear the bird weep, flying as it always did in the chill rain. Then he would see his mother crouching in the dark on the dirt floor in front of the house keeping vigil. 'What karma has condemned the wretched creature to be chained to the fate of being born without the ability to make its own nest?' In the relentless downpour of the night rain the bird's song could be heard approaching and then diminishing, and each cry was punctuated by the mother's laments and sighs.

The expression of the mother's concern for the bird went beyond words. One day she transplanted a camellia sapling in the corner of the small plot in front of their house and began tending it with the utmost devotion. In the depths of winter no one could have waited for the spring's arrival as fervently as she did for the sake of her camellia. Only when the tree bore beautiful and pristine buds, showing that it had survived the fierce cold, did spring finally arrive in his mother's mind. Her concern for the tree and her impatience in waiting for the appearance of spring were not just driven by a desire to see the flowers but by her need to provide a shelter for the rain-bird. During the summer and autumn, on mornings after nights of the bird's incessant plaintive cries, she paid even more attention to the plant. Early in the morning she would inspect it and sprinkle millet around it for the bird. Even though she knew that camellias were unsuitable for planting near houses she had chosen this particular tree because its leaves were abundant and large enough to make a snug home for rainbirds.

The boy had never seen the rainbird and did not know what it looked like. All he knew about was its song. The mother, too, had never laid eyes on the weeping birds.

'What's the point of knowing what they look like?' she would say. But she continued to feed any bird that flew to the tree. And numerous ones flew in from the rain to rest in the camellia branches, consume the millet seeds and take off. It would have been impossible to speculate which was the rainbird, but the mother didn't seem too concerned about finding out.

One day, however, it became clear what a rainbird looked like. It turned up in the form of the elder son who had left home, like a kite separated from its string. He had attempted to earn a living in the city. He had sent no word home since then. Since his mother had spoken only rarely about him the younger son had no idea what his older brother looked like and had no idea if he was still alive. But the brother came home after thirty years, penniless and exhausted.

The mother showed no resentment at her son's pitiful homecoming. 'What byways have you groped you way around all these years? Where did you shelter from the wind and the rain at night?' All she could do was continually caress the roughened hands of her son, who had grown old even before he even had time to bloom in her eyes.

'No, Mother. I did not suffer. Away from home, out there, I met many older women, who like yourself had seen their sons leave home. It was because of their kindness that I was able to return home safely,' the man said calmly, comforting his parent. 'Come to think of it, for too long I have not been a good son. Look at that camellia. There was no tree there when I left home, but now it's huge,' he said, his voice tinged with regret.

Inexplicably the boy saw the rainbird in this man. In his brother's remorseful homecoming he conjured up the image of the bird with its mournful cry, flying endlessly in the rain, looking for a place to rest, its tail limp and head drooping from exhaustion.

'Although my mother rarely mentioned her elder son, in her heart she was always talking about him. To her, he was the rainbird. That's what I am trying to tell you.' The host concluded the tale of the rainbird that had so affected his childhood. He then went on with the story of what happened to his brother after his homecoming.

'So it may not have been the real name of the bird. My

mother might have just made up the name "rainbird", as she listened to the bird's cries and projected all her longing and her hopes into its song.'

The elder son soon realized the magnitude of his mother's devotion to him and began to plant trees everywhere around the house, perhaps to make up for the pain he had caused her during his long absence and in order to demonstrate his love for her. He bought more land near by and planted a still greater variety of trees.

He suffered from the sickness of wanderlust, however, and he left home once more, this time when the saplings he had planted had grown into substantial trees. One late autumn day, soon after his aged mother had drawn her last breath while resting her head on her son's knees, the brother was gone. It was as though he had been waiting for her to die so he could leave after having accomplished what he had intended to do – to build his own nest.

'I've heard nothing from him since. He may no longer be of this world. If he is still alive, how could he do this to me?' A sad smile surfaced on the farmer's face as he spoke somewhat resentfully. He picked up the cup and drained it and then began his confession about the mistaken identity – that he had seen an illusion.

'The strange thing is – you may not believe this – occasionally I seem to see him coming back here, unable to forget his trees.' Again he assured his guest that he was aware that his brother would never actually come home once more. He had stopped expecting him, and now he no longer tried to listen out for the rainbird's cry. But, in spite of himself, he sometimes saw the bird among his trees.

Now the traveller began to grasp what his host was telling him, and at last he understood why the farmer had waved.

'Please forgive me, but when I saw you standing there I thought it was the bird again. Ah . . .' The host sighed, which could have been an apology or self-mockery; the traveller was unable to tell.

The guest had in fact anticipated what the man would say, and there was no reason for him to respond. He remained lost in deep respect for the man. Yes, the farmer had become a tree; that's why he looked like a tree himself, he thought. He was the rainbird, and the host was a tree in the wood. The bird saw the tree, and the tree again saw the bird. The traveller understood why he had felt such a peculiar sense of comfort as he stepped into the home of a stranger.

After all, the whole thing had started with the man the host called his brother. As the host had said, the rainbird had been nothing more than an imaginary creature conjured up by his mother because of her longing for her son, and the orchard that had lured the traveller was the work of the brother. The farmer's desire for his brother's return, just as deep as his mother's had been for her son, would sometimes cause him to spot the rainbird among the trees.

What the farmer was waiting for was the real person and not the imaginary creature. However, his brother would return to his wood only as a rainbird. Just as the man's mother had planted a camellia tree not only for a single rainbird, for her son, the farmer provided resting places in his woods for all the bone-weary travellers who were also the rainbirds of his childhood. His brother might have ceased to reside in his mind. What he saw among the trees was something more real and not a hallucination. The farmer had become the tree that watched the bird.

It was an amazing and precious relationship.

The traveller found himself lost for words, feeling too deep a gratitude for the strange twist of fate that had brought him and the man together at the end of his long journey. Silently he drank cup after cup of wine, basking in his own languid, peaceful mood. He felt he could go on drinking all night.

But the traveller discovered that the story of the rainbird was merely a prologue. Revelling in the karmic encounter, he had incorrectly surmised his host's intent. More importantly, he had forgotten about his own affairs. His thoughts had not reached far enough to fathom the man's reasons as to why he had talked at such length about the rainbird's search for a nest. For the time being he had lost track of his own wanderlust and of what it was that he was looking for, just as he had been unaware of the host's true motive for telling his tale.

Meanwhile the host appeared to have read the traveller's mind, that his guest, too, was aware he had another motive in telling the story of the rainbird. The tale he had so far related had a deeper meaning than the traveller had comprehended, which had something to do with the traveller's background and what he did for a living. This had become clear to the guest as the host once more surprised him by returning to the subject of the wretched rainbird.

So far the host had not asked his guest's identity, as if he already knew all he needed to know about him. His silence implied there were more things to be said and that he was searching for the right words to begin to say them. The way he passed the wine cup wordlessly to his guest indicated that he was waiting for the traveller to make the first move.

At last the traveller intuited the host's situation, but he was unable to find the words to respond because he couldn't work out what the host wanted to hear from him. Then it occurred to him that in order to continue the conversation the host had to carry on. He pondered. The farmer had evidently not yet finished telling his story. There must have been many more tales of birds that had flown into his woods, and some must still be there. This man would make sure his woods were always occupied. The guest was willing to wait for the host to tell their stories. He must remain a silent listener until then.

The traveller had found no need to initiate the conversation once more, but in order to coax the host to continue he decided that he must make the first move and ventured, 'I would guess there has been more than one bird you let in, just as today you invited me into your house.'

'Yes, indeed, dear sir. You are not the first.' A faint smile of disappointment appeared on the farmer's face.

'Then would you please let me hear about them, if you still remember some of them?' urged the traveller to encourage the host to carry on. At this point the host began to show signs that he was letting go of some expectation he may have had of his guest.

For a while the farmer did not speak, merely nodding a few times. But soon, regaining his composure, he agreed to comply with his guest's request.

'Certainly, if that is what you want,' he began. 'You would be mistaken if you thought there had been many such stories. As you know, not everyone who happens to pass by my woods is a rainbird, but there is one particular person I must tell you about – the bird that disappeared last spring.'

The host seemed to be hurrying into the story, as if he had been ready to tell it all along, and it immediately grabbed the traveller's interest.

'I think it was in the autumn four years ago.'

Once again he began to unravel the skeins of a tale that had begun one autumn dusk, the story of one peculiarly pathetic rainbird.

The farmer had been getting his trees ready for winter late in the day, as he did every year. When he looked up towards the mountain behind the woods he noticed a stranger wearing Western clothes smoking in a sunny spot on the slope. He was puzzled because he seldom saw people up there. Since the stranger remained in the same position for a long time, barely stirring and gazing down at the meadow, the farmer turned back to his work. A few hours later, however, he looked up and saw the man still sitting in the same position smoking cigarette after cigarette. And, until sunset, each time the man looked up the slope he would find that the stranger had not moved at all throughout the entire afternoon.

The farmer was perplexed. He did not want to go up to the stranger and ask why he was there, but he found himself thinking about the man on the hillside and could not concentrate on his work as long as he remained on the same spot. The sun was about to set, and he began to worry that it would be dark soon. To his relief, the stranger disappeared from the slope where the dark shadow had settled.

But the farmer soon discovered that the stranger had not departed from the village, for he saw the shape of a rainbird about to enter the gate to his orchard. Upon closer inspection, he noted that the stranger was shabbily clad and bore an expression of peculiar weariness. No doubt, he must have seen his long-gone brother in the stranger, the bird that he had always associated with his brother's appearance.

Without first making enquiries, he invited the man into his home for the night. The farmer learned that his guest was not a stranger to this part of the country and that he had left his home town in the region as a young boy and had been living in different cities. The guest said that he was a writer of poetry but confessed that he did not actually know what a poem was. He went on to say that although he understood a person who wrote poetry was called a poet, he would rather call himself a poetry man, a humble artisan of words. He had written so many praising his southern birthplace that his name had come to be known among even those who did not understand his poetry or anything about him.

This poetry man, however, had grown weary of city life and had begun to look for a plot on which to build a house away from the city. He had found a place to his liking on that day, a parcel of land where he would be happy to build his house, and that was the reason the farmer had seen him there. When the poetry man had decided to move to the country, he thought the move should be to the village where he was born, where his umbilical cord was buried. Although born and raised in this region, because his entire family had moved from the region he had no relatives or acquaintances to help him after so many years.

He told his host that he had no more energy to go on looking and asked him whether there was any way that he could acquire some land on the slope. He had no resources to build a house immediately, but, if possible, he would purchase the land and build the house later when he had had a chance to make some money.

The host assured him, 'Very well. I'll see what I can do to help.' Something in the poetry man's story had touched the farmer's heart, and he came to a decision immediately.

Had the land belonged to him, the farmer would gladly have given a parcel of it to his guest for nothing, but it was owned by someone else. The following day he went to see the owner. Everything went well. After listening to the farmer the property owner gave him his consent, saying that if the price was right there was no reason why he would begrudge the buyer a plot for a house. And so a deal was struck between him and the poetry man. A million won was the sum agreed upon for a parcel of land measuring about a hundred square metres, a sum slightly below the going price of a piece of land of that size.

'Until you decide to build the house, I will start planting trees for the border of the property and in the yard. I will use the trees from my own woods.' The farmer volunteered, excited by the satisfactory conclusion of the deal.

The real problem was what happened afterwards. The poetry man had no resources to pay for the land. He did not even have enough to pay a deposit for the contract, let alone one million won.

'It's difficult for me right now, but if you could wait for five or six months longer at most I'll have some other means to get the money,' he pleaded, embarrassed at having to confess this after all the time spent bargaining. He said he could not raise that much money at that point even if he were to sell everything he owned. But a job was waiting for him in the city. He had realized he could not make a living by writing poetry and had accepted an assignment to write a biography of a wealthy industrialist.

'It will take me five or six months at most to finish it. I'll come back with the money. I promise you.'

The poetry man left only after repeating his promise to the farmer. However, in the end, the deal had ended merely as a verbal contract.

The land owner, somewhat puzzlingly, had consented to the verbal agreement and even permitted the farmer to plant trees on the property.

The farmer waited six months, planting trees in the meantime, but heard no word from the poetry man, not even a letter asking for more time.

From the beginning, it was not because he had made a promise to the poetry man that the farmer had trees from his land growing on the plot of land; the project had been entirely his own initiative. Yet he began to think it futile to go on and that the deal he had helped to make could go sour. The farmer stopped planting, and thoughts of the poetry man began to fade from his mind.

One late summer afternoon, however, more than two months after the six-month period had passed, the farmer again saw the man sitting in a sunny nook on the slope in the same position he had been the first time, once more smoking. He had held back from going up to meet the poetry man but waited for his next move. And, just as before, the poetry man came into the orchard at dusk, looking like an exhausted rain-bird, and without challenging him the farmer invited him in and provided him with a place to rest, knowing straight away that he had returned without the money.

As expected, the poetry man admitted that he still did not have the cash; he could not finish the biography. He promised that if the land owner would be good enough to wait a few more months he would certainly manage to finish it. Once again, the farmer and the man spent the night drinking, and the following morning, with a vague promise just as before, the poetry man left to return to the city. The farmer no longer believed in the man's agreement and knew that he was incapable of writing the biography of the business mogul and that he had given up the idea altogether. The poetry man must have known that his host had already worked this out, and this knowledge put his mind at ease.

At his next visit, the promise to pay for the land was not kept, just as before. The man came back without the money and left after spending a day with the farmer and making a renewed commitment to bring the money next time. However, the poetry man did not say when he would next return. Since that time he would come and go whenever he felt like it. When he returned, after spending all day sitting in the same spot, he would appear in the orchard like the rainbird that came in from the rain and let the farmer provide him with a warm place for the night. Each time he would promise to come again, and the farmer, encouraged by this, would resume planting trees. The poetry man would not give up his hope of owning the land, and the farmer had become used to him and his empty words and continued to plant trees on the plot.

The farmer did not believe that the poetry man was actually capable of writing someone's biography and had long ago abandoned the hope of his returning with the cash. By then he had become used to the unreliable habits of the poetry man, and he had no desire to rebuke him. He was happy just to let him stay overnight in his house and to plant trees on the land the poetry man had no hope of owning.

Then, during the spring of the previous year, the poetry man returned to the village once more. This time he told the farmer to stop planting trees after spending an afternoon on the mountain slope. 'No use. Please stop it – I mean you planting the trees,' he said helplessly, as though this plea was meant as the payment of the debt he owed the farmer. The farmer felt a strange premonition in his behaviour. However, when he considered their relationship, which had never been intimate, he refrained from asking the reasons, fearful of intruding on the man's private affairs, and he pursued the matter no further.

The following day the poetry man left without a word of explanation or a promise of return. Even after his departure the farmer could not get rid of the peculiar sense of foreboding, for he had never seen the man act that way before.

There was to be no more news from the poetry man, and the farmer's premonition was to prove tragically correct. A month went by, then two, and a long time afterwards, enough time for the man to have paid a couple of visits under the usual circumstances, but still he had not returned. The farmer could not endure the ominous presentiment and sent a letter to the his address in the city, which, fortunately, he had kept. He received a reply from the man's family, informing him that his friend had died about six months earlier, soon after his last visit.

'He was the bird, the wretched bird who never made his nest. He died without ever owning the land he so desperately wanted for his own.'

The traveller had been listening without touching the wine cup until the host's story came to an end. Knowing how much the poetry man had desired the land, the farmer decided to buy a small portion for him to be buried in, the plot of ground in which he had planted trees. He sent a letter to the man's family to let them know of his intention. They wrote back, telling him that since they could not find a proper grave for him they had already cremated his body and scattered the ashes over a river, as had been his wishes.

'His remains were blown over the river. The fellow never had a place of his own, even after his death. I wonder if his soul transmigrated into a rainbird and keeps coming back here now, for his wishes were unfulfilled during his lifetime. When I saw you first this afternoon, a thought occurred to me. I don't know how you will take it, and I am sorry to say this, but it was not only my brother but the poetry man that I saw. That's why I waved at you the way I would at someone I know. I used to wave at him just like that when he came. It had become my habit. I would not do that to just any stranger.'

The dead and the living . . . And after the tangled account of the bird and the human beings the host finally concluded his story. He drained the wine from his cup and gazed expectantly at his guest for a reaction.

But the traveller remained silent. He sensed that the farmer already knew everything about him. The rainbird had been a mere prologue to the story of the poetry man, and the story of that man was not about the rainbird, who was for ever unable to find a place of his own. The host was talking about the traveller himself.

The host must have already had an insight into what the traveller was seeking, but he waited for his guest to reveal it of his own accord and did not pressure him into a discussion. It did not seem important for him to know whether his guest was willing to talk about it or not, because he had already, in his own way, alluded to the issue in his oblique way.

Then the awful thought occurred to the traveller that the land the poetry man had so fervently desired was not for the living but for the dead. This, too, must have been clear to the farmer. There was nothing for him to explain, no need to say anything about himself if the host already had access to his thoughts.

They continued drinking, but their conversation lagged after a while, there being nothing much more to say to one another except scraps the host remembered about the poetry man. It was past midnight when they decided to go to bed.

The traveller was unable to sleep until daybreak. The events of the day had kept him awake. He was exhausted, feeling the weariness of the poet's lifetime was now transferred to his own body, and its weight pressed down on him, making him limp like a water-soaked cotton ball. At the same time his thoughts were becoming more lucid.

'He said that he had become tired of a life bound by *nunchi*, the social skill of intuiting other people's minds or assessing a situation,' the host had answered when the traveller asked why the poetry man had wished so fervently to live in the country. People understood *nunchi* to mean something that facilitates relationship, and life was no more than a continuous search for a means to achieve harmonious relationship between 'I' and other people. It was a clever argument, and no one had to remind him of it. He had already experienced it living in the city, a life overcrowded and complex, and he had become horrendously tired. The city dwellers were so preoccupied with creating hollow, useless relationships that they lost their true faces and their own places. Relationships people so arduously sought to establish were not sound when their only purpose was to serve personal interests; they became relationships that merely engendered exploitation and domination. In the process, people sold their true natures and forfeited the right to their own place in the world.

He remembered what the host had said earlier about education. The host said that people flocked to cities with a fierce desire to get an education. Education, according to the host, was nothing but to teach one the game of *nunchi*. For them, education did not mean people learning how to find themselves or places for themselves but the passing on of skills and greed that would maximize their abilities to compete with and control others. Thus, they had ultimately created a society wherein everyone had burned himself out in an effort to read the intentions of others as a means to win in the game of one-upmanship and domination. Those without their own faces and places of their own could create only empty relationships, and ultimately even the masters of the *nunchi* game could no longer survive in such an environment.

Was there any place on earth where one could find such a place, where one did not have to think about relationships? Wondering this, the traveller now realized that his long years of wandering had harboured a desire, hidden even to him, that he meet someone whose life did not depend on creating superficial relationships. He finally found a sense of kinship with the poetry man's desperate search for a place of his own in a remote rural area away from the life of *nunchi*. He wondered if the man had found respite from this weariness in the host's disorderly orchard.

He realized that it did not much matter whether the poetry man had actually been able to buy land to build his house during his lifetime. What mattered was that in the woods he was finally able to release himself, albeit only for a short time, from the yoke of relationships bound in terms of possession and domination. He, too, felt the poet's desperate desire for his place still lingering in the orchard, and this feeling was most natural to him. In the orchard he finally found the true form of an honest man, something he had lost and for which he had searched all his life. The farmer was the first and the last real person whom the poetry man had encountered in his life. The farmer's life represented a solitary existence, free from compromise and free from the need to forge profitable connections. His refusal to build such relationships allowed him to be sure of himself and be faithful to his true nature. Freedom from ownership extended beyond human relationship. He refused to possess even a single tree.

The traveller remembered the host's remark when he had asked what had happened to the trees he had planted on the poetry man's land. The man's reply was: 'I left them alone there. I see no reason to dig them up and move them somewhere else. Even a blade of grass has its own life, and that life doesn't belong to me. People tend to manipulate living things, moving them around at will, because they think they own them. If you tamper with other's lives, yours will be also be tampered with. Human beings as well as trees must stay where they belong, each in its own place. A tree has rights just as it has life.'

Man and tree, each to its own, that was an exquisite relationship . . . The farmer refused to claim possession the life of even a single tree, abstaining from the creation of a forced relationship. In this way he allowed himself the freedom to create his own place and to maintain harmony between himself and his trees. One could not force this harmony, it could happen only when one was secure in one's own place, and without it no encounter and no relationship were possible.

The poetry man must have found his sense of security in the intimacy between the man and his trees. Although unable to own the land, he kept coming back because of this realization. In the orchard and in the farmer he found a brief respite from the accumulated weariness of his life.

But in his room at night the traveller could not become like the poetry man. In place of relaxation, the weariness that the other man had shed in the orchard entered his body, weighing him down, controlling his mind and body, keeping him awake.

What kept him awake was not remembrance of the wretched life of the poetry man, nor of his ending as a handful of ashes scattered over a river, but thoughts of his strange method of shedding his life's burden. And, worse, the field songs the poetry man had listened to while crouched on the slope of the mountain kept him awake through the night.

The host had said that the poetry man had an amazingly

keen ear for the songs of this southern province, and he wondered if it was a common trait among poets and whether the man himself had been aware of this gift. When the traveller had asked why the poetry man had coveted that particular spot on the slope of the mountain, the host's answer had been 'He told me that he could hear the songs. Sitting there he heard the rise and fall of farmers' songs, the songs they sang while they worked in the rice paddies. And he did not move until sundown when the songs were heard no more.'

The traveller asked the farmer if he had ever listened to the poetry man sing. To this, the host replied that the fellow was no singer himself. The farmer wondered whether it was because the poetry man was from this southern region that he was so fond of the local songs. He once asked him to sing for him, but he adamantly refused. When he persisted, with a bit of cajoling, he reluctantly complied.

'He sang a modern song, a song currently popular among children, which went something like this – you know the one I mean – it begins with "White cloud hung over the distant mountains" and ends with "The sun's last glow, red flame over the western mountain". The man sang the refrain over and over again, mustering all his efforts. I tell you, you wouldn't have wanted to hear his voice more than once,' he said, shaking his head.

It did not matter to the traveller whether the poetry man had a good voice or not, but the man refused to leave his thoughts; he remained sitting on the sunny slope, searching for the songs of the fields. And the traveller found himself wandering together with the man in his search of songs.

The next morning the traveller overslept in breach of good manners. An eerie silence filled the house; he assumed that breakfast had been consumed and dishes washed. The host must have ordered the household to be careful not to awaken the guest. The traveller was embarrassed to be heard stirring in his bed and remained idling there for a while longer. The late autumn morning sun suffused the paper window with soft white. Only then did he gather up enough courage to emerge from his room. The sun had already risen high, indicating that it was almost lunchtime.

He saw the host and his wife working together in the orchard, once more protecting the trees from the frost, and the son had left for his work. The couple noticed him and came out of the orchard. 'You needed to recover from the exhaustion of your journey, so we let you sleep. You must have been tired.' The farmer's morning greeting sounded like an apology.

Together the host and his guest walked into the yard. The farmer pumped water from the well into a basin for the guest who cleaned himself with fresh cold water to rinse away the heavy burden of his thoughts.

When they settled in the inner room the wife brought in a simple breakfast table.

'You must feel very uncomfortable from last night's drinking.' The farmer, who had the strong constitution of which country folk boast, offered more drink to his guest, insisting that the wine would help him to get over his hangover. This time the lids of the rice bowl were used as cups. The host, having spoken, now fell silent. He showed little sign of interest in his guest's agenda or his background, thoughts or reactions to their conversation the night before.

The traveller had nothing to say either; he had heard everything there was to hear. If there were anything that remained for him to discover he would have to hear it from the poetry man, the rainbird, and not from his host.

The two rushed to finish their breakfasts like men with urgent business to attend to and set out together for the path through the wood – as if they had promised one another that this was what they had intended to do that day.

They walked towards the poetry man's parcel of land. During the night the traveller had made up his mind to see it. He decided he must see the piece of earth that had offered the respite the man had sought for so long. He must hear the strains of farmers' songs rising from the field, not only for the sake of the poetry man's soul but for his own. He saw no need to tell his host about this and asked for no companionship. Yet the host followed him in silence. Both men knew where they were heading. Because of the effect of the wine with breakfast he felt even the host's presence to be intrusive.

By the time they reached the gate of the wooden fence that enclosed the orchard, the traveller felt compelled to say to his host, 'I'd rather go there alone. You must have a lot of things to do. I don't want you to trouble yourself on account of me.'

The host understood, for his guest's demeanour conveyed a determination that was not to be ignored. He studied his guest for a few moments and then gave up the idea of accompanying him. He nodded a couple of times and pointed his finger in the direction of the poetry man's plot.

'As you wish, my dear sir. It's over there, on that slope. Do you see that patch surrounded by trees?'

The traveller did not need directions. He had already noted the place as they came up from the path. 'Very well. I'll have no problem finding it. I'll see you later.' He strode away from his host even before the man had finished giving directions and stepped on to a ridge between the rice fields leading towards the mountain slope.

The property was not far from the orchard, and the

traveller reached it in no time. Young, hardy orange trees were growing abundantly along the edge of the land, and within it many varieties of fruit trees and saplings of garden shrubs flourished, some six or seven years or so old, some seemingly transplanted within the previous year. An open area in the lower part of the plot was probably intended for the house. The vacant portion gave a solitary and melancholy air to the place, a suggestion that it was not a happy spot for a new house to be built but more a site where a building had been demolished long ago.

At the bottom of the gently sloping hill the traveller found a clear area in the corner of plot. He settled down there and lit a cigarette.

So, this is where he would sit all day long, he thought as he began to take in the surroundings.

He found nothing particularly remarkable about the landscape, certainly nothing to excite the viewer, except perhaps for the whistle of the breeze that rose from the pine grove in the mountain ridge behind the property and the warm rays of sun that shone on the field. He thought also that the clear view below of the field, from where farmers' songs that the poetry man was said to have listened to drifted up, justified the price of the land. He looked down on the farmer's orchard, beyond which was a broad expanse of farmland, lying fallow after harvest. The late-autumn fields offered him no comfort; he could hear no farmers' songs and not a soul came into view. But he remembered that the poetry man would sit here and wait all day long, coming down only after sunset.

He was beginning to have doubts about the man's reasons for desiring the land so intently. What was he looking for here? Was he deluding himself? Had he overestimated of what the land could offer him? Would the poetry man actually have found relief from his weariness even if he could have found the money to buy it?

He could not dislodge thoughts of the man. The story he had heard the night before preoccupied his mind. He hoped his soul had found peace, and, if possible, he wanted to uncover evidence that the man had found it in this place. He blamed his ears for not hearing the songs. He opened up the ears in the deepest recesses of his mind and directed them to the farthest reaches of the fields, waiting with a fervent hope to hear the songs rise once more, those farmers' songs that the man had heard.

Look here, my dear farmers . . .

He could think of no finer example of a farmer's song than the one from *Chunhyang Jeon*

He remembered the song that the young master Yi had encountered in the fields of Namwon. But then, during the rice planting seasons, one could hear these songs from anywhere in the southern provinces:

In the large fields, we plant late-maturing rice.
In the furrows, we plant early-maturing rice.
In the highlands, we plant dry-field rice.
In the paddies near our houses, we plant glutinous rice.

He waited expectantly for the seeds of the songs from his peripatetic life to germinate once again in this special plot of land. For a long time he let his thoughts drift over and reach the fields of all the regions where he had journeyed in search of songs.

Look at that flock of geese,
Moving jauntily sideways like a crab's crawl.
Our bowls are packed high with rice like a soldier's helmet.
Our cups overflow with barley wine.

Then, as he let his mind unfold over the landscape of his life spent chasing the songs, gradually his ears began to pick up the faint refrains of the farmers' songs, teasing his senses, weaving between the whistling winds. Finally, the songs, overcoming the rustling of the pine wind, resonated in his ears, penetrated his body:

Once, twice, three times we weeded the fields
Under the burning heaven of the hottest month of summer –
And, after all our hard labour is over
We pray for a plentiful harvest, and
For the five types of grains to ripen,
Their heavy heads drooping down.

The songs grew louder, permeating his body, filling its every crevice as it diffused following the wind towards the distant fields that stretched below his vision. Aroused by the approach of the songs, the field began to show signs of stirring, and farmers began to surface, as in the landscape of a dream. From everywhere, like sun streaks, the farmers' songs rose up, from the whistling of the wind, from his own body and from the fields. The songs rocked his body and soul gently into a state of hazy repose.

The sun's warmth embraced the surroundings, and, with the soundless chorus in his mind, the calm of the desolate plot began to unfurl its wings. Time had stopped. He had become oblivious to the sun's transit and deeply engulfed in a singular sense of comfort. He traversed far and wide, wherever the songs led him.

Songs were everywhere, in the whistling wind through pine groves, in the nameless white cloud-shrouded green mountains, resonating at every turn of the road of his life's journey.

He had become the songs, soaring over heaven and earth.

The comforting sun coaxed him into a nap, and he still heard the songs in his sleep.

Suddenly, a blast of cold wind awakened him from his long repose. The sun had already gone down, and the dusk was beginning to settle. He could not shake off the delirium of the dream, and the songs that had filled his ears had disappeared from the winds and from the evening fields. Instead, the sombre whistles of the wind riding over the mountain ridges replaced them, ushering in the night. The soft dusk enveloped the empty fields of late autumn and began to recede from his blurred vision.

Then the traveller at last found the songs again. He was about to leave just as the lost songs flowed once again into his empty heart. He stared at the last flourish of sunset filling the western sky with its flaming crimson hue:

> The scarlet flame of the sunset . . .
> The scarlet flame of the sunset . . .

He remembered what the host had said about the poetry man's wretched effort to sing the song of setting sun, and in that scarlet flame he could once again hear the forgotten songs:

> Please come back. Can't you come back . . .

He was now listening to the poetry man's modern popular

song, the anguished song of the sunset, because the poetry man was incapable of singing the real songs, the pansori of the south:

Today, as ever, the sun hung in the western mountain
Burning in a scarlet flame.

The poetry man had become the song. The songs had never ceased; neither had they ever disappeared. He and his singing had become the flames of the setting sun.

With these thoughts the traveller slowly descended the mountain.

The host met the traveller at the gate to the orchard. He had not wished to interfere but had been anxiously waiting for his guest's return. He had already decided the traveller would leave him before nightfall.

'Well, I thought so.' The farmer's response was simple when his guest had expressed his gratitude for his hospitality and gave notice of his imminent departure.

The guest hesitated for a while, feeling compelled to say a few words of explanation before taking leave of the host, about the fact that the man had been considerate enough to leave him alone, asking no questions to the end.

'You have been very thoughtful. I am embarrassed to leave without having made up my mind.' His apology almost suggested a promise of return. 'I may return one day, if the opportunity presents itself. Please don't think of this as an end, for I will need your help when I come back next time. I am sure you already know. This piece of land impressed me favourably.'

Once more the host had guessed the traveller's thoughts and did not believe his guest's polite words. 'There's no need for an apology. There are those who could not stay in a place even if it pleases them. My brother, for instance, had to leave home after planting trees and hoping to live to see them grow into a grove.' A smile of resignation surfaced on the farmer's face as he spoke, for he knew for sure that his guest would not return, just as his brother had not.

The traveller found it hard to leave. To help him get going, the host asked his guest, 'So where are you heading now?' It was the first question the host had posed since the traveller had entered his house, but the traveller could not answer because he did not have a clear destination in mind. In his mind he could see the roads along the seashore he had travelled before coming here, where sun's rays broke the waters into incandescent waves. Recently he had travelled through regions close to the sea where it had been easy to find songs. But now he had no thought of returning to the sea again. He had already seen a sea where there was no seawater and heard songs of the inlet in which the sea no longer entered. Everywhere, up on the mountains and from the earth, he heard the songs of the south: one who could not hear those songs was not a southerner.

'I have no particular place in mind. If I could get a ride to town I might look for a place where I could find a pansori singer. You see, I am a lover of pansori,' he said somewhat sheepishly as he started to move off.

The host understood and mumbled, 'A place where you can hear pansori singing? Let's see now. I wonder nowadays whether you can still find somewhere . . .'

He followed a few steps behind his guest and added with a hint of reproach, 'It's entirely up to you, my dear sir, and none of my business what you are looking for; a place of your own or the songs. But, as I see it, you are the songs. Why do you persist in looking for songs when you are already carrying them strapped to your own bare back?' The host's comment none the less betrayed a profound empathy for his guest.

'Well, as you say, there might not be such a place any more,' he lamented, pretending he had not comprehended the host's remark. 'But it doesn't matter now. When I look at the sunset's blaze, the red flames, I cannot remain in one place. So long, stay well and in peace.' And, without waiting for the farmer's words of farewell, the traveller left as casually as someone who was planning to return soon, and he hurried towards the horizon where the western sky glowed with the setting sun.

The host found himself falling out of step with the traveller and finally stopped completely. Now he, too, had become a tree, holding the dream of the nightbird that had just left the nest it once called its own, watching the figure of his guest grow dimmer as it moved towards the sunset.

THE REBIRTH
OF WORDS

A GROUP OF schoolchildren was descending the mountain path, with their transistor radio blasting out a song with bizarre lyrics: '*Ka, na, ta, ra, ma, pa, sa . . . pa, ha . . .* so many more words I wish to say'.[10]

Kim Seok-ho stepped aside and waited for them to move on. Ji-uk, who was following closely behind him, also paused to recover from the uphill climb and took a deep breath.

'Cheon is heaven, *Ji* is earth; *hyeon* is dark, and *hwang* is yellow.'[11]

The party, equal numbers of girls and boys, moved on, paying no attention to the two men who stood at the edge of the road to leave the path clear. They marched on impetuously and happily, singing the lyrics of the songs the men had found weird and which also sounded a little like folk songs.

Kim and Ji-uk waited silently, gazing up at the snow-covered summit, until the singing youngsters had disappeared into the woods below. They exchanged a look of disenchantment, which contrasted sharply with the jolly marching songs the schoolchildren were singing as they moved down the mountain trail.

'What were they singing?' Kim asked in bewilderment. He couldn't believe his ears.

These were the first words Kim had spoken since they had passed the road sign on the gate of Pyochungsa Temple about ten minutes earlier. The sign read 'Iljiam 2 km'. The uphill climb had been too hard to encourage conversation. Still, Kim appeared to be a man of few words. Ji-uk had noticed this the day before when he had first met him. Kim gave only cursory answers to the questions Ji-uk asked and had been silent during the car ride to Daeheungsa Temple. Since they had left the car in front of the temple and started on the path leading to Iljiam they had not exchanged a word. Ji-uk thought that Kim must have been so offended by the youths' song that he was forced to break his silence.

Ji-uk knew very well what Kim meant, but he rephrased the question anyway, 'You mean, what were the kids singing?' He took out a cigarette and lit it. 'They're the latest pop songs.'

'But what do the words mean? They're almost like Buddhist chants. And why do they recite the Chinese characters from *A Thousand Characters* and the Korean alphabet?' Kim did not smoke but moved on, ending his words with a deep sigh.

'That's not all. They recite anything: the list of dynasties, numerical tables,' Ji-uk added.

Kim looked like a man buried deep in a thicket of words, seldom emerging – at times he looked like a solid block of words, so that his wordlessness matched his immobility. However, when he asked Ji-uk had detected a hint of animation in Kim for the first time, but after that he reverted immediately to his impassive self. Ji-uk's intention was to hold on to the tail of Kim's words and use it to pull him out of his silence. But Kim's trail of words had already disappeared, dashing Ji-uk's hopes. Kim did not stir for a while, keeping his gaze fixed at the sky.

Ji-uk read Kim's silent lament, as if to say, *It's the end of the world. Yes, it is definitely the end. Even children are turning themselves into idiots.*

Kim started to move again, walking feebly. Ji-uk followed closely behind conducting a one-way dialogue in the hope of getting a conversation going as he waited for Kim to speak again.

'You can't just dismiss them as idiots. In a way, we can assume it's the form through which they speak their language. We occasionally mask our true meanings in form rather than in the content of the words – the form becoming the words, so to speak.'

Kim moved on without answering. He was not a man to be persuaded easily, but Ji-uk had grown accustomed to his silences and learned how to respond to them, for he realized Kim substituted responses with his silences. Last night, while Kim remained indifferent, Ji-uk found himself trying too eagerly, perhaps, to engage him in conversation. But now Ji-uk was able to see little worth in the words Kim uttered, and he stopped himself from becoming too interested in his companion.

'Crying and laughing are the most elementary means of self-expression. We read sentiment and alterations of mood by their forms, or modes, of expression alone even before we understand what it was that inspired the cries and the laughter.'

Ji-uk almost shouted his argument at Kim's silent back.

'Poetry and songs are more advanced, but still the form is the message, preceding content. I believe people depend even more on the form of expression when the essential content of what they say lacks ability to persuade or arouse sympathy.'

Still there was no reaction from Kim.

'At least, that is what I think. Chinese characters or numerical tables are not the content of lyrics the schoolchildren were singing; they are but the form. Therefore, those who sing the songs knowing this cannot be idiots.'

As he spoke, Ji-uk felt pained. This was the only way he knew how to defend the living words of this generation and their principle.

But Ji-uk was used to being disappointed. He had endured enough disillusionment over words: words that had lost contact with objects, words bereft of substance, words whose content no longer carried a message, words without any basis of meaning, words whose survival depended on the form they represented. And he had attained a certain tranquillity of mind from having gone through these recurring experiences of disappointment.

Ji-uk could not guess whether Kim had understood his mood. Kim showed no reaction and walked on in silence. Suddenly Ji-uk began to think that it had been a mistake to go to Iljiam and that he had misjudged Kim, whom he had hoped to be a man with deep interest in and understanding of the nature of words. It was, then, for nothing that he had come on this strenuous uphill journey following this man.

Ji-uk was a writer. He had written biographies of famous people and had ghostwritten the memoirs of many others. In the process he had suffered complete despair over words. He had stopped meeting up with his fellow writers, those sad word-craftsmen and, secluded in his house, had spent days contemplating and reading in search of a means of rediscovering words that were yet unspoiled.

One day he had made a discovery, a rare and precious find, a book entitled *The Selected Works of Choui*, edited by Kim Seok-ho of Namhae, Jeollanam-do Province. It was a translation of the works of a renowned monk, Choui (1786–1866), who lived during the reigns of King Jeongjo and Cheoljong and had written in Chinese.[12] The book was a selection of poems and two essays: one was entitled *In Praise of Korean Tea* and the other *A Chronicle of the Tea God*, which set out the basic rules of tea-drinking taken from the Chinese *Encyclopaedia of Ten Thousand Treasures*. What had captured Ji-uk's attention were the tea-drinking rules mentioned in the essays. The code of tea-drinking that Choui introduced in his work was as follows:

> The Tea Scripture says, tea is the god of water, water the body of tea. The god does not appear in water that is not pure, and water does not manifest the god if the tea is not pure . . . It is when the god and the body are equally present that harmony of spirit and body is achieved . . . As to the brewing method, when the water has just come to a boil, pour a small amount of it into a teapot to take the chill out of the teapot and then discard it. After this, place an appropriate measure of tea leaves into the teapot and fill it with just-boiled water. Too many tea leaves will produce bitter tea, making the taste inferior, and too much water will dilute both the colour and the taste. If the water is too hot, the tea god will be injured. A clean teacup enhances the spirituality of the water. Allow the tea leaves to steep, then pour the tea through a piece of hemp cloth before drinking it. If the tea is steeped for too short a time, the tea god has no time to appear; if too long, the aroma is lost . . . The gathering of the tea leaves requires infinite finesse and processing them infinite devotion. The water must be pure, and the brewing must be balanced to achieve a state of constant equilibrium. When body and god are equally present, and being and soul merge together, the Tao of tea is attained.

In this description of the Tao of tea Ji-uk discovered a maxim capable of governing the relationship between spirit and words. The spirit, or reason, would take the place of the tea, the god of water, while words, the field for the operation of reason, would take the place of water. Just as an excess of tea leaves would spoil the fragrance of the tea and too much water would fail to bring out its colour and taste, an imbalance of mind and words would adversely affect both, leaving the mind without fragrance and words without colour or flavour. To put it another way, in the writing of Choui on the Tao of tea Ji-uk read something more – a principle that governed words as well. He was fascinated by this extraordinary monk because he believed that Choui had defined the principle of tea-drinking partially with other objectives in mind. He discovered a deep humanity in his discourse on tea and believed it was what Choui must have intended when he wrote it.

Choui was the pen name of Chang Ui-sun, whose enlightened learning embraced both the Confucian classics and Seon Buddhism and who excelled in poetry and painting.[13] He was intimately acquainted with the giants among the Buddhist monks and Confucian scholars of his day and with whom he exchanged poems extensively. *The Selected Works of Choui* was devoted largely to the translation of the poems that had been written in Chinese, especially those exchanged between Choui and Cheong Yag-yong (Tasan, 1762–1836) and Kim Jeong-hui (Wandang, 1786–1856), renowned scholars with whom Choui had shared scholarly interests and the pursuit of the Tao. He was especially close to Wandang while Wandang was languishing in Jeju Island having been banished from the court. Choui had planted and cultivated Korean tea, also known as 'Sparrow's Tongue tea', so named because the leaves were picked when they were very young, at the height of their flavour and no larger than the size of a sparrow's tongue. He so loved the tea that he wrote *In Praise of Korean Tea* and *The Chronicle of the Tea God* in an effort to revive the tea ceremony, which was on the wane in Korea at the time.

If Choui was so vigorous in his mind and enjoyed such a

wide circle of eminent friends, then one might ask why he had cultivated the habit of solitary tea-drinking. Tea-drinking conjures up in the mind an occasion for sharing the joy of the free exchange of ideas among close friends. And yet Choui shrank from such gatherings. He wrote:

> When drinking tea, the smaller the company the better. Too many companions spoil the refinement of flavour. Drinking alone is divine, with two is excellent, with three or four it is a pleasure, with five or six it is an offence and with seven or eight it is a waste.

No doubt his discourse on the Tao of tea reflected his particular introspective reasoning. It would seem that the mental discipline he had achieved by observing the ritual of tea-drinking had enabled him to conceive a wide range of thoughts, giving birth to numerous poems and the terminology of the tea ceremony, such as *essence, control, purity, body, divinity, soul, equilibrium* and so on.

His effort to maintain temperance and a sense of equilibrium in his view on the spirit and words was demonstrated in his poetry:

> The epistle you have sent to me through Heo So-chi[14]
> Preceded the flock of geese flying in the autumn wind.
> I urge you, let us live in mutual oblivion.
> Only in oblivion does one attain emancipation from torments;
> Only in the absence of torments does one attain Tao . . .

He wrote this poem in response to a tea poem he had received from Cheong Hak-yeon, a son of Cheong Yak-yong.

Simply put, the principle governing Choui's tea-drinking

was to maintain the equilibrium of words and spirit. Just as the god of tea manifests in the codes prescribed for tea-drinking, so did his words give birth in the temperance of his spirit.

Reading the book, Ji-uk had a sudden urge to visit the place where Choui had lived and, if possible, to seek an encounter with a few still living words.

He set out to visit the author Kim Seok-ho in the south without any particular agenda and with only a vague hope that Kim might be able to offer him more information about Choui. He wanted to know the author's motives for writing the book and the reason why Kim tried to recreate the tea-drinking rituals that Choui had mentioned in his writings.

It had all started when Ji-uk had come upon a short magazine article written by Kim Seok-ho concerning his thoughts on the *Selected Works of Choui*. It was this magazine article which had initially inspired him to read the book itself. In the article, Kim stated that he had laboured assiduously to master the Korean tea ceremony. However, he never managed to achieve the enlightenment experienced by Choui and found no clues in Choui's writings to an understanding of the Tao of tea.

Ji-uk was intrigued by Kim's motive for editing Choui's works. He was also convinced that the author must know something, however nebulous, about what Choui was searching for in the rules of tea-drinking. Ji-uk wanted to observe first hand Kim's struggle as he searched for what Choui must have sought in the Tao of tea for, by witnessing it, he, too, might be able to help satisfy his own longing to discover the fate of the lost words.

But Ji-uk found this southern man to be quite the opposite of what he had expected. Although he had taken a great deal of trouble in coming so far to meet him, Kim expressed no pleasure when he arrived. Moreover, he did not seem particularly interested in tea and had, in fact, dismissed Ji-uk's enthusiasm for *The Selected Works* as nothing more than idle curiosity.

Ji-uk asked Kim his opinions about drinking tea simply to keep the conversation going while leafing through the pages of the book.

'Have you read that book? If you have, follow what is written there.'

Kim did not mention the doubts he had expressed in the magazine article. Moreover, throughout the evening he had not invited his guest to join him in the sipping of Sparrow's Tongue tea, although Ji-uk hoped for at least as much from a man who was celebrated for his expertise in the art of drinking this special tea.

At every opportunity Ji-uk would press for information, but Kim would either pretend that he had not heard the question or would avoid giving a straight answer.

'I came here believing you are a man with special expertise concerning the nature of words. I also believe you have attained your knowledge by going through actual experiences. I would like to hear about some of them.'

Although Ji-uk spoke unequivocally about the purpose of his visit, Kim dodged his repeated queries, allowing no interaction with him. Ji-uk's impression of his host was that his words and thoughts were bound together without a slightest hint of movement

The following morning, however, Ji-uk discovered that Kim was not completely without thoughts of tea.

'What do you say? You came all the way here. How about some tea this morning?' After the breakfast table had been taken away, Kim said, 'Tasan believed the best time for tea-drinking is when one wakes up in the morning, while observing a cloud float past in the clear blue sky or after a midday nap, and when viewing crystalline moonbeams breaking into pieces on the surface of a stream. I can add one more: after a sleepless night with a guest, while gazing upon the night snow that carpets the front garden of a thatched cottage. Not bad for an exercise in the art of drinking tea. Ha, ha.' The sound of his voice lingered, accompanied by his laughter, which Ji-uk had rarely heard till then.

Overnight snow had fallen, and the exquisite quiescence of it covering the front garden must have prompted Kim to desire tea. He brought out the paraphernalia for brewing it and began to prepare for the complicated procedures he had described in his book.

When the tea was ready Ji-uk noted that Kim did not follow his own strict rules as he savoured it. Kim wrapped his hands around the teacup, almost the size of a bowl, and sipped the lukewarm beverage slowly and sparingly, like a man who had just come in from the cold. Not satisfied with one vessel, he drank cup after cup. He appeared indifferent as to whether Ji-uk observed the etiquette of tea-drinking and merely continued to fill his companion's cup, seemingly oblivious to anything but drinking his tea.

Since Ji-uk was obviously unacquainted with the ceremony, Kim's indifference to the formality of tea-drinking put him at ease. At the same time, the expectation he had nourished began to fade. He was beginning to think he had come for nothing. Had it not been for the invitation Kim was about to extend, he might well have decided to return to Seoul after the tea-drinking session was over.

'If you are not pressed for time, would you like to visit Iljiam?' Kim had asked casually.

Iljiam, which was a Buddhist hermitage in the compound of Daeheungsa Temple, was about fifteen kilometres from the town of Haenam. The monk Choui had died there at the age of eighty after a life dedicated to the pursuit of learning and of the Tao of tea. Recently the members of the Tea-drinkers' Club in the Haenam region, in which Kim held a high position, had restored the hermitage to its original condition. It was considered to be the place where anyone interested in Choui and his tea should pay a visit, at least once in a lifetime, as should those curious about whatever enlightenment Kim had sought in Choui's writings on tea. No doubt Kim must have had all these things in mind when he extended the invitation, and Ji-uk, too, sensed a special significance in the offer.

'It snowed, fortunately. There is a person who will welcome us there, a monk who can tell you some real stories about tea.'

There was a subtle hint in Kim's remark that, unless he had misread the younger man's mind, taking him there would relieve him of the necessity of talking. Ji-uk found no reason to hesitate, and they set out immediately on the road to Iljiam.

Ji-uk had no illusions that going to Iljiam would answer all his questions and entertained no hope of being enlightened by the monk, who according to Kim was well versed in the Tao of tea. He had not come this far to learn about the tea ceremony – he even doubted whether he would be able to understand a connoisseur's discourse – what he hoped was that he would at least learn Kim's motive for taking him there, which might help him gain some insight into Kim's thoughts on words. Kim alone held the key to the questions, Ji-uk believed, regarding what had happened to words we use, which he thought Kim was keeping deep inside him.

Kim, on the other hand, remained impervious, seemingly

still unable to read Ji-uk's mind, even unaware of his own motive for taking him to Iljiam.

It was past lunchtime when they finally arrived. The one-kilometre climb was arduous but well worth it once they reached the hermitage. They had been unable to pay much attention to their surroundings while they struggled upwards – the narrow path through the woods was completely obliterated by the snow – yet the hermitage in its snowy setting struck them as a landscape fit for immortals. There were two buildings situated on an elevation in the compound, the sanctuary of Buddha and next to it a pavilion, a thatch-roofed structure reconstructed from the original one in which Choui had resided. The snow had accumulated on the roofs and on the tea plants in the courtyard. The silence and tranquillity of the scene sent a chill to the innermost recesses of a visitor's mind. For this reason many urban scholar-painters were known to come here to immerse themselves in the snow-clad views of Daeheungsa Temple. Ji-uk thought that the view had made the trip worth while even if Kim had disappointed him.

'Is anyone inside?' Kim enquired feebly while facing the closed door of the sanctuary.

In doing so, he failed to observe the proper etiquette required for a visitor, and his manner was no more refined than that of a villager passing by the brush gate of a stranger's house.

'Why so much snow this year?' he grumbled to no one in particular, as a middle-aged man in Buddhist garb emerged from the backyard with a broom for clearing snow.

'Indeed. The road must have been quite slippery.' The Buddhist, too, spoke as casually as one would to an acquaintance of long standing, his palms pressed lightly together in the Buddhist greeting.

Ji-uk was puzzled. The Buddhist betrayed no particular

interest in the stranger who accompanied his acquaintance, merely directing his pressed palms in his direction in lieu of a spoken greeting. Ji-uk saw that he must be the very person Kim had mentioned as the monk who could enlighten him with the true story of tea. He sensed the trusting relationship between them and speculated that their friendship needed no formality, thinking this might be the way they normally introduced people to each other.

'We have come a long way. How about some tea for us?' Kim demanded abruptly, feeling a chill in his bones.

'Certainly.' The response was just as casual. 'Have you ever brought a guest here with any purpose other than to drink tea? When I saw the heavy accumulation of snow I thought to myself that you might come today. I have been waiting.' The monk looked at the two men as he was about to leave before adding, 'I'll prepare the tea. Go inside and make yourselves comfortable.'

'I am here not because of the snow but to introduce to you a guest who has come on a long journey. You ought to brew a special tea for this special person,' Kim called out to the disappearing monk.

Ji-uk thought the remark out of character for Kim, and then it occurred to him that coming to Iljiam had put Kim in a peaceful mood.

'I am no judge of his sutra chanting, but when it comes to tea, he is truly enlightened.' Suddenly Kim was ready with words, imparting an impression that as he became comfortable in his surroundings his words, too, began to flow with ease.

'It seems that you two need no formality between you.' Ji-uk seized the opportunity and tried to coax Kim into conversation.

'I come here to beg for tea whenever I have time.' This time Kim's response to his remark came without delay. The change in Kim's behaviour was obvious. 'I have also brought my guests here before, as I did today,' Kim added without being asked.

Then, forgetful of the monk's suggestion that they go inside and unmindful of the cold, Kim began to study the snow-covered valley below.

'Do many people come to ask you about tea?' Ji-uk ventured cautiously. He was not now interested in the invitation to tea or in the monk's discourse on tea. He must keep Kim talking.

'They keep coming, just enough to ease my boredom.' Kim's voice was low, but there was no sign of reticence in his answer

Ji-uk continued with his questions, no longer hesitant. 'What do they want to know about tea?'

Kim brushed snow from a stone step and sat on it. 'Let me see. Most complain that the rules of tea-drinking are too difficult and that even if they do follow all of them they are still not quite sure they really know how tea should taste.'

Kim then cited an example. The previous summer about twenty members of a city tea society had come to see him. They were on their way to Daeheungsa Temple on a sightseeing tour. Without exception, they had complained it was too much trouble to follow the rules and asked him if he had a trick he could share for making the tea-drinking ceremony less of a hassle. Instead of telling them what they should do he brought them to Iljiam.

'No doubt the rules are important. One can achieve enlightenment in the Tao of tea only by following them. However, the spirit of the drinker lies beyond such formality. We often completely fail to understand this and insist instead on the process alone to reach it.'

Kim went on talking at an easy pace, his gaze still fixed on the valley below. As he listened, Ji-uk realized that Kim was not as awkward with words as he had thought him to be at first. What Kim said made sense, and, moreover, Ji-uk detected a trace of unfamiliar passion. Gradually Kim began to relax the rein that had restrained his words and to unleash his own spirit as well by setting his words free. Until that time there had been no movement in what few words Kim had spoken. He harnessed his words tightly to himself, allowing no interactions with the listener, so that Kim himself looked like a person without movement. But now, with his words freed, Kim let himself move closer towards Ji-uk, which caused him to suspect that Kim had thus far been saving his words, waiting for this very moment.

'Are you saying that Iljiam teach them to see something beyond formality?' Ji-uk pursued Kim with his question, as he remembered that Kim had shown scant regard for the rules of tea-drinking that morning. It occurred to him that what the members of the tea society were looking for and what Kim had wished to show them without words, and what he himself was searching for, were the same thing. Kim must have had this equation already in his mind from the beginning. 'Here in Iljiam the great monk Choui sipped tea until the day he died. But the reason I brought them here was to introduce them to the monk you saw a while ago. I told them he could tell them something about tea. I can only mimic the monk.'

In this remark, Ji-uk read Kim's real motive for bringing him to this place. Introducing him to the monk, as Ji-uk surmised, was an excuse. The truth of the matter was that Kim himself had something to say and show to Ji-uk. Without intending to, Kim betrayed his thinking by telling Ji-uk the story about the members of the tea society. Ji-uk did not let Kim know that he was aware of this but continued instead to question Kim in an effort to discover what Kim wished to reveal.

'Do you mean to say that the monk Choui himself did not insist on the rules of tea-drinking?'

'I believe he did not towards the end of his life.' Kim raised himself from the stone step, looked around and, while methodically brushing snow from each branch of the surrounding tea plants, continued, 'Choui was eighty when he died here. In those days, when a person reached that age he would have been almost blind and deaf. But in spite of his advanced age he remained here alone and brewed and sipped his tea. So, do you think he, with those conditions, would have been capable of following the complex formalities of the tea ceremony, even though he was thoroughly accustomed to performing them? I have a feeling that he burned his fingers on the charcoal fire because of his failing eyesight and at other times spilled the water, losing his balance. I imagine that after a great deal of effort, if he finally succeeded in brewing the tea and taking the cup into his hands, I see him sipping the tea slowly while viewing the valley below with dimming eyes. Do you imagine he obeyed the rules? I suspect he sipped the tea only with his spirit.'

'Then,' Ji-uk pressed on, 'what do you think was in his mind at those moments?'

Although Kim was about to hit the bull's eye, he suddenly changed the target. 'I wonder. I cannot explain it in a single word. Even I, who believe that rules are not everything, find it the greatest of enigmas. I struggled for many years to master the difficult rules of tea – no less rigorously than those members of the tea society, I assure you – but I found that there is no single word that can explain the real taste of tea. All the effort I put into it became meaningless. In my heart, the words of despair kept repeating themselves. I am aware that there must be something we cannot arrive at by following form, but I was not able to figure out what that something might be. So, I came here as often as I found the time to do so, seeking enlightenment from the monk. I wanted to know how Choui took his tea, what he saw and what he thought while sipping tea. I came again and again in the hope of discovering some residue of the master's spirit buried here in this place, a clue that would reveal his thoughts to me. I came all the time. I came when seasons changed, on rainy days and when it snowed. I came sometimes by myself and at other times with guests – just as I did today. All this I did because I needed to find the answers to the riddles of his mind.'

'So have you found the answer then? What did you show the members of the tea society, and what did you tell them?'

'Nothing.' Kim shook his head, dashing Ji-uk's expectation, and added, as though to offer an excuse for disappointing him, 'Since I myself had no answer to the riddle, I brought them here so that we could find it together.'

'Did anyone find the answer then?'

'No.' Shaking his head again, Kim sighed in deep resignation. 'Some compared it with poetry, some associated it with Buddhism and some others thought it was a meditation on life. But not one of these explanations made any sense to me. What they said was all nonsense.'

'What is the basis for your conclusion that it is all nonsense?'

'It was because they could not experience for themselves what they talked about. If Choui contemplated a poem while he sipped his tea, we, too, ought to be able to enjoy a poem while drinking tea. If his mind dwelled on Buddhism and found in it a meditation on life, it must be possible for us to do the same. I believe that as we drink tea we must also encounter the mind of Choui. Yet while we can only imagine, we are never able to meet his mind through poetry, Buddhism or the meditation on life. If that is so, while these words might define Choui's way of tea they cannot define ours. And, if we fail to grasp his authentic thought and experience his joy of tea-drinking, then poetry and the rest would become mere abstract formality, just as meaningless as the cumbersome rules of the tea ceremony. Believing this, I had no choice but to send those who came to me for advice to the monk at this temple. I had to let them know also that the Tao of tea is such that a mere monk could not enlighten them. Although he knows much about tea, he can only tell them to search for the meaning within their own minds.'

Once released, Kim's words flowed out in a jumble. Separated from him, they sounded no different from those of any ordinary people.

'Then did you bring me here today just to test your theory out on me?' Ji-uk demanded to know, forcing Kim into acknowledgement.

But Ji-uk misread Kim. Kim had not lost control of himself. On the contrary, because he was so sure of himself he had digressed only to lead Ji-uk on and all the while had been patiently waiting for the moment when he could reveal his final single word to him. He had the answer in his possession and had merely been groping his way through the forest of idle words to access it. But he was not yet ready to release the rein that held it in check.

Kim remained silent despite Ji-uk's urgent challenge, without taking his gaze from the snow-covered valley below. All his movements were suspended; the hands that had been dusting the snow from the leaves of the plant were still.

Ji-uk heard Kim speak slowly behind him. 'Do you see that town below? See some of the inns there? One day last year, after a visit here, I met a strange traveller in one of them.'

Kim was now oblivious of Ji-uk as he continued speaking of his encounter like a soliloquy.

'I was resting in the inn – the Yuseon Inn – when I heard a man walk in somewhat hesitantly. I overheard him ask whether anyone knew of a female pansori singer in this area. People here are still fond of pansori, but it's been an age since a tavern or inn retained singers to entertain customers. I thought it odd that someone should go around looking for a pansori singer today, and I became curious and asked him the reason for his request. I ended up spending the night listening to the story of his search, his strange, desperate tale, his wandering life in his quest for the songs of the south. I learned that the man worked for a traditional herbal medicine business in Seoul. His job was to collect medicinal plants, but that was just an excuse for him to travel seeking for the pansori of the south. He told me that there was no place he had not roamed looking for them.'

'He must have been a true lover of songs,' Ji-uk interjected impulsively. He knew almost nothing about the style of singing called pansori. He had not had much opportunity to listen to those songs that were no longer heard in cities today, and he had no real opinion about them. He was not excited by that kind of music, although the song's deep resonance and dignity were evident even to his ear. Still, he could not help himself from becoming curious about the traveller's strange obsession, just as Kim had been.

While his gaze rested on the valley below, entranced by his

own narrative, Kim did not heed Ji-uk's interruption, and he continued, 'I spent the night drinking with the traveller. When I woke up late the following morning, the thought of tea suddenly came into my mind. As you must know, nothing can cure a hangover like Sparrow's Tongue tea. But I don't believe it was because of the hangover that I suddenly craved tea; the traveller's tale stirred my desire for it. I don't know how to explain it, but for some reason, when I listened to his story, his wandering in search of songs, Iljiam surfaced in my mind. I must take him there, I thought. As soon as we had eaten a meal to ease our hangovers we left the inn. Of course, the traveller came with me, following me even before I had mentioned my idea to him. Only when we reached Iljiam did I finally realize why I had wanted to bring him here from the first.'

Ji-uk remained silent.

'On our way up there we lingered in the compound of Daeheungsa Temple, so by the time we finally reached Iljiam the day was almost at an end. But we were not in any hurry. Neither he nor I had any particular schedule to keep. It was a fine day, so we just sat in the open, exactly as we are now, and sipped tea without exchanging words. Time dragged slowly, in part because he did not seem especially fond of tea and was unacquainted with the proper manner of tea-drinking. He sipped his tea in a leisurely manner, regarding the valley below and deep in thought.'

Ji-uk continued to listen in silence.

'He looked to me to be about fifty years old. I read an extraordinary weariness in his expression and in his movements, a frayed spirit under his shabby appearance. And as he sat sipping his tea, gazing motionlessly down into the evening valley, I suddenly saw the image of the monk Choui. It occurred to me that Choui must have sipped his tea just the way the traveller was taking his. That's what I thought. I couldn't analyse why, not then. I believe that he affected me in the same way the southern songs had compelled the traveller to wander all his life. I saw in him the root of the ethos of our existence, and I suddenly encountered Choui's way with tea, a revelation all by itself.'

At last, Kim emerged from the forest of tangled words and was about to reveal their nestling place. Ji-uk waited silently in anticipation of the moment when Kim would finally display the contents of this nest.

'It was a strange karma, my encounter with the traveller. I have written books about the tea ritual, and I have been drinking tea according to the rules. But I learned the truth about it from someone who had nothing to do with such things.' Patiently and deliberately, Kim was approaching the final revelation. 'It was useless to deny it, but I read with absolute certainty the spirit of the Choui's tea-drinking in the traveller. What's even more certain, as I watched him I felt something engulf me with heat, the fire that scorched the depth of my heart. I shall never forget this experience.'

'What was it? What was it that dwelled in Choui's mind while he drank his tea?' Ji-uk could not hold himself back any longer and pressed for a final answer from Kim.

As though he had no more words left, Kim spoke in a low voice, looking steadily at Ji-uk. 'It's forgiveness. Nothing else.' This sounded more like it was intended to convince himself rather than his listener.

The Buddhist had been ready with his tea for a while but had refrained from interrupting the two men engrossed in conversation. At last he reappeared and urged the men to follow him into the room where the relics of Choui were kept and offered them the tea. Mesmerized by Kim's story, Ji-uk had not realized that he was chilled to the bone until the tea warmed him with a remarkable feeling of comfort. Kim must have shared the same warmth that the tea offered. He again drained cup after cup of tea in rapid succession without respecting the decorum required for tea-drinking like a man craving something hot.

Ji-uk was not at ease. He was unacquainted with tea etiquette, but he was also reluctant to repeat the way he had mimicked Kim that morning.

'One feels more comfortable following the rules than doing it one's own way, it seems to me,' Ji-uk confessed, feeling somewhat embarrassed.

Kim responded as casually as if he had been expecting this remark, 'We agree that it's troublesome to follow the rules, but it's even more difficult to transcend them. To attain the state of mind that makes it possible to drink tea without adhering to the formality of rules is, I assure you, not easy.'

Kim paused a while, thinking he had rushed through his point too quickly and continued to clarify what he had just said. 'To forgive others, yourself and the whole world and to be thankful; this act of forgiveness is easier said than done. I, for one, have come here many times but can only pretend to know it. I know of no other person but the monk here who can drink tea with true understanding.'

Then Kim told Ji-uk to go ahead and drink his tea in a way that felt right to him and to ask the monk any questions he might have.

'You repeat your idle words, Mr Kim . . .' the monk protested. 'I refuse to participate in your affairs again. I wonder how many times have I been forced to say absurd things on your account.'

Ji-uk found himself losing interest in tea. It was not so much that he minded the monk's sermon on the taste of tea as being found only in one's own mind but that he was unwilling to endure yet another idle discourse on tea. The words of the cognoscenti were too esoteric to a layman such as he. He wanted rather to hear the rest of the story about the traveller that Kim had begun to tell him, the story of a man who spent half his life searching for songs.

Ji-uk did not really understand what Kim had said, that ultimately the Tao of tea was analogous to finding the capacity for forgiveness in one's life and that he himself had come to Iljiam repeatedly in his struggle to find the way to that forgiveness.

Ji-uk, however, felt it was too abrupt a transition; Kim had rushed from discourse on tea-drinking to the traveller. Now he realized that Kim brought up the story of the song-obsessed traveller only as a clue. He wondered what forgiveness meant to Kim, to Choui and to the traveller. What was it in the life of the traveller that taught Kim the meaning of forgiveness? What did Kim find? And having found it and with his knowledge, what drove him repeatedly to visit Iljiam like a pilgrim? The truth, he thought, must lie in the circumstances of the traveller's fervent search for songs. But Kim had skipped that part of the story.

'Naturally, atonement and then redemption should precede forgiveness,' Kim went on. 'And finally gratitude. It must have required a great deal of effort for Choui to brew tea; he must have spilled water, and he must have burned his fingers. In my opinion, when he sipped his tea, gazing down on the valley with his failing eyes, it is unlikely that he would have been thinking about the ritual of tea-drinking. He might have been contemplating poetry or Buddhism. But I believe he was meditating on the transitory nature of the concerns of his own life and pondering the meaning of atonement, redemption and thankfulness in his interactions with countless other human beings he had encountered in his lifetime. He might have asked himself whether he had wronged another human being or caused others to bear grudges against him. Finally he must have felt grateful for that state of mind he had attained through repentance for his transgressions, a forgiveness of himself and deliverance from guilt.'

Kim's discussion about 'forgiveness' was only a supplement to the understanding of Choui's Tao of tea, but Kim had not said anything about the traveller who had helped him to reach this conclusion. Yet Kim mentioned that he was still unable to experience this process in his own tea-drinking. He only pretended to understand it, something only Choui and the traveller shared.

Ji-uk realized that, through tea-drinking, Kim sought to experience this very state of forgiveness himself. But Ji-uk was not yet ready to interrupt him, no matter how impatient he was to learn more about the traveller. He waited for Kim to finish his tea-drinking session.

Ji-uk wondered if Kim had already read his mind or if it was how he always behaved. At any rate, Kim lingered over his tea until Ji-uk became tired of waiting. Kim's silent tea-drinking, however, released Ji-uk from the burden of having to listen to further talk about tea.

It was not until the winter sun began to set and the two men began their descent down the mountain path that Ji-uk attempted to resume the conversation about the song-mad traveller.

'I assume there was a special reason or event in his life that had turned the man into the lover of pansori? I mean the songman you mentioned earlier.'

Save the occasional thuds of snow falling from the heavily

laden branches, a deep calm shrouded the mountain temple in the fading light of late afternoon. Without uttering another word, Ji-uk followed Kim down a slippery path through the woods, where the snow had frozen to ice.

Kim's answer came only after they had arrived midway through the wood on the way to town, but all the while it seemed that he had been thinking about it himself.

'I didn't say "songman". A lover of songs looking for songs, but he was not a singer himself.'

Kim's response sounded like his conversation with Ji-uk about the traveller had continued uninterrupted, and he had known that this was exactly what Ji-uk had been thinking.

'Yes, one most heart-wrenching event. It was precisely because of it that I wished to take him to Iljiam.' Kim had clearly reserved this for this moment. He intuited the urgency in his companion's silence and no longer ignored it and added, 'He told me about his childhood.'

What the traveller had told Kim was that he had a half-sister with an exceptional voice, a gift she had inherited from her father, himself an outstanding singer. The father had taught his daughter to sing and had trained the traveller, his stepson, to accompany her on the drum as they travelled from village to village.

All the while they moved about, however, the drummer boy was plotting to murder his stepfather. The boy hated his stepfather because he believed he had killed his mother, and he was determined to avenge her death. Yet from the beginning it was a hopeless scheme, for he was neither strong enough nor clever enough to carry it out. Moreover, the stepfather's songs had begun to enrapture the boy, sapping him of his will to carry out his secret plot. As time went by, the boy feared more and more that his love for the songs would eventually cause him to forgive his stepfather, to desire to become a drummer and ultimately to choose for himself a life like his stepfather's. One autumn day this fear finally drove him to run away from his half-sister and stepfather. He had to hide himself from those haunting songs that had bewitched him in order to preserve his hatred for his stepfather and his desire to avenge his mother's death. From that day until he reached middle age, he lived a solitary life without receiving a single piece of news of his stepfather and his half-sister.

Then, strangely, after many years, when he thought he had completely forgotten about his stepfather, the memories of him resurfaced in his mind. Soon he found himself on the road, visiting places throughout the southern provinces in search of songs.

By that time, almost thirty years had elapsed since the day he had run away, so that there was no reason to believe the stepfather would still be alive, and he had few means of finding out about him. However, he clung to the belief that his half-sister was still living and drifting from place to place to sing the songs of her father, songs of primal pain. Yearning and with ardent hope, he had travelled everywhere during the past ten years looking for her and her songs.

'Why do you suppose he began to think about his stepfather and half-sister after all those years, when he had already lived half his life? And why did he try so hard to find her?' Kim posed these questions in concluding the traveller's story.

Following a few steps behind Kim, Ji-uk remained silent. They were about to leave the dank, slippery wood and to enter a narrow path with a smooth surface descending from the northern hermitage. Then, just as the level path began to ease his steps, the meaning of the word became clear to him. Ji-uk had paid a high price to experience its depth and history, by struggling with doubts, making mistakes, groping and stumbling in the dark.

The traveller's odyssey was to seek reconciliation and forgiveness, to repent the grudges he had borne against his stepfather and for his scheme to kill him, to atone for his heartless abandonment of his young half-sister. But the traveller continued to live in regret, for he no longer had the means to find the two people, those from whom he sought forgiveness and whom he could forgive had gone.

Ji-uk finally understood Kim's motive for telling him the story of the traveller. It was to illuminate the meaning of forgiveness in order to lead him back to finding an answer to the riddle of the mind hidden in the tea-drinking.

The going had become easier as the path became smoother. Kim began to walk briskly away from Ji-uk, which might have been an indication that he had posed his question to Ji-uk neither to measure his ability to understand nor to extract an answer from him.

For his part, Ji-uk lost patience. He found himself rushing his steps, feeling the weight of the word *forgiveness* pressing down on him now that Kim had unloaded on to him the meaning of the word and the events in the traveller's life. He was unable to bear the burden of that single word. To lighten the weight and in the hope of being altogether free of it, he asked, 'Has he found his half-sister, then?'

The answer was the opposite of what Ji-uk anticipated.

'Yes. He told me that he had received news of her whereabouts and had gone to see her.'

'Then his wishes must have been finally fulfilled.'

Ji-uk thought that Kim's voice betrayed the ease of someone about to conclude a story, but Kim said only, 'It could have been possible only if it was what he wanted.'

Again Kim's response was negative, but he spoke as lightly as if he were about to unburden himself of his last piece of baggage on to Ji-uk.

'But, no, it was not what he wished it to be, as I understand it. His half-sister was living somewhere in Jangheung singing in a tavern. When he finally located her he was unable to reveal his identity to her. And the woman gave him no sign of recognition. He listened to her songs, and they parted as strangers.'

'It took him so long and so much trouble to find her. Why didn't he tell her who he was?' Ji-uk pursued.

It was not hard for Ji-uk to understand that after spending half his lifetime in search of his stepfather and half-sister the traveller might have found it difficult to reveal his identity. Perhaps the idea of reconciliation had become meaningless to him by then. In any case, he had found what he had been searching for. Yet, if this was all, his many years' of wandering ought to have ended by then, but it had not. Even after finding his half-sister the traveller still continued his interminable quest for her. Why? Ji-uk could not find the answer, so he put the question to Kim.

This seemed to be precisely what Kim was waiting for, and he answered immediately, 'I suppose it was because of her songs.' He spoke calmly, as though the weight he had been bearing alone for so long had finally been lifted. He relayed to Ji-uk the last part of the traveller's story.

'You must have already guessed it. What were her songs? People often talk about the southern songs as expressions of *han*, a perpetual and profound pain. But in a truer sense, I see the songs as capable of exorcising all the pain of our lives, turning tragedy into the resolution of *han*. Although others say that to sing these songs are to amass the *han* in our lives, but I believe otherwise, that they have the ability to comfort and ease all of life's woes, to unravel the tightly tangled knots of *han*. Those whose lives are entangled in *han* sing to rid themselves of it; for them it is to live. Such was the case of the woman. When the traveller finally located her he found that she was blind. She sang to live, and her songs had become her life. Her blindness aside, what was the *han* that had committed her to singing? I doubt that her half-brother was solely responsible for her suffering. I suppose that when he saw what singing had become to her he could not announce his identity to her; her songs had become her life, the songs to disentangle the knot of *han*. What's the use of talking about repentance and forgiveness? These words meant nothing to them any more.'

Kim paused, not to wait for a reaction but to steady himself to deliver the conclusion of his story.

'The traveller came to understand something else as well. At least, I think he did. It was this, that even if he were to beg for forgiveness from her and attempt a reconciliation, even if she were to hear his confession, they would still have to go their separate ways. They would have to go on living, seeking their share of penance and forgiveness. It was for this reason, I believe, that he gave her up and left. Even now, he depends on the songs to pay for his share of the debt. I have a feeling that from the beginning the search for his sister might have been merely an excuse.'

When they finally reached the town at the foot of the mountain it was dark.

'Let's find a place to warm ourselves,' Ji-uk suggested. He had no reason to accompany Kim further and no desire to accept more hospitality from him that night. He wanted to be alone after a few drinks with Kim somewhere near by and let him go. Kim seemed to have the same idea. He led Ji-uk to an inn, an old-style building where one could get drinks as well as accommodation.

The sign on the building that read 'Yuseon Inn', and Ji-uk realized it was the one in which Kim and the traveller had stayed. Ji-uk wondered whether Kim had brought him there for some reason other than to provide him with meals and lodging for the night.

A middle-aged woman who seemed to be the proprietress greeted Kim effusively and suggested, 'I assume you want your usual favourite room in the rear building?' Even before she received an answer, she led them to a quiet room in a separate building behind the main house.

Kim bantered with the woman as he followed her, calling out, 'I need a drink right away! I am hallucinating, I see ghosts.'

The proprietress made sure that the room was in order and was about to leave when Ji-uk heard Kim make a peculiar request. 'Is she here now? I want to see her comb her hair tonight.'

'Do you hear me? A wine table for our guests, right away! They say they're seeing ghosts!' Her shout came even before her steps died away. 'Hasn't our precious princess Seon-hui finished combing her hair yet? If her ladyship hasn't, tell her to finish it in the guests' room. Mr Kim is waiting for her there.'

Ji-uk found it difficult to understand the meaning of 'princess' and 'combing her hair'. Was Kim referring to a girl who used the care of her hair as an excuse for her laziness? Why should Kim request service from such a girl? Ji-uk contemplated these matters for a few moments but felt no particular curiosity to pursue it, and Kim did not give him a chance to dwell on it.

'Well, it has been a hard day for you, and it's all been for nothing, hasn't it?' Kim asked as soon as they had settled comfortably in the room. He did not actually mean that Ji-uk had not benefited from the experience; neither did he mean to ingratiate himself with his guest. He meant only to express relief that the expedition was over. For him their trip was about to come to an end.

For his part, however, Ji-uk could not dismiss Kim's comments and felt compelled to express his gratitude for what he had learned during their trip. 'No, please, don't think that the trouble has been for nothing. I have learned and gained much.' He wanted to say more, but Kim interrupted him.

'There was not much I could show you, and I doubt that you learned anything, but you tell me that it was worth while, and I am relieved to hear it.'

Ji-uk interpreted Kim's remark as an indication that he wished to terminate the exchange and feared that to go on thanking him would only prove to be an empty and embarrassing gesture. Still, he felt that he had a debt to pay, and so he continued to speak, even if Kim was indifferent to what he was about to say. 'As I was telling you last night, I have been searching for the nature of words, words that really matter. I don't mean those words that have departed from our daily lives, the dead words that exude a stench around us. I want to encounter living, breathing words, words in which we can put our faith.'

'Then have you found them? Where?' Kim asked without much conviction in his voice. Whatever words he had uttered heretofore – the words he had set free – were now once again ready to retreat to their captivity. Kim himself was now ready to resume his reclusive bearing, becoming once again the impassive man Ji-uk had taken him to be the previous night. He acted like a man who had forgotten everything, even his own motive for taking Ji-uk to the mountain temple. He showed no interest in what Ji-uk had hoped to gain, in what he had found there or in the words that he said he had finally been able to comprehend.

Ji-uk, however, needed to conclude what he intended to say and went on. 'I am talking about Choui's favourite Sparrow's Tongue tea. Did you not tell me that blindly following rules is merely formalism, that rules empty of life are not true rules? I believe I can say the same about words. Those who try to reach enlightenment in the tea ceremony and the seeker of the southerners' songs are all dedicating their lives to the search for the same word, *forgiveness*. It was through them, this very fortunate word, was reborn over and over again: for Choui in the spirit of his tea-drinking, for the traveller in his sister's songs and for you, I assure you, in your faith in another human being.'

Kim did not respond.

'The word, that single, blessed word, has gone through repeated rebirths, never losing faith in itself.'

Again Kim said nothing.

'But what I mean to tell you is this: I, a man who is unable to bear the weight of even that single word, cannot dare to claim I discovered it.' Ji-uk paused. He no longer wished to continue, although there remained more yet to be said.

He had been thinking about the freedom of words. This generation was suffering from the effects of a terrible revenge that was being inflicted upon it, a rightful retribution we human beings deserved for their betrayal. We mistreated words so that they had lost their faith in themselves and were floating around seeking vengeance. On this day Ji-uk finally saw the possibility of encountering the words that had not chosen the way of revenge and witnessed the existence of words that had endured the throes of countless rebirths and metamorphoses and still maintained their integrity. He had also realized that the roots of these words were entrenched in the lives of human beings, engendering in them a capacity for reconciliation, the meaning of which was life itself.

A word that had not chosen the way of revenge had so endured the process of metamorphosis that it was now beyond recognition in its original form, and its meaning had become multifaceted and surreptitious. Only by thus under-going transformation of form, however, could a word survive and maintain its integrity, and only through reconciliation attained at the price of great suffering could a word achieve final emancipation. Life becoming words and words life . . . He pondered if a realm of the words existed, the words that represented life itself, offering a possibility for them to be free . . . This was the final truth about the nature of words that Ji-uk had gained in the temple that day.

Ji-uk kept these thoughts to himself, realizing it was meaningless to go on with his discourse with Kim. Only now did Ji-uk reach this clear insight that Kim's indifference so far was not because he had not been listening to Ji-uk but because words had ceased to be useful to him.

'I wonder whether there are other guests on a cold day such as this,' Kim mused. Then, seizing the opportunity to deliver himself from an awkward silence, he quickly switched his attention to the wine table that had just been brought in, eye-ing it with the expression of a person in great need of food.

What was presented was not a simple wine table but one large and elaborate that reflected the formalities of classical Korean cuisine not commonly found outside refined restaurants. It was no wonder that it had taken so long to prepare. A young woman followed behind the person who carried in the table, apparently the girl Kim had requested. She wore a traditional

Korean ensemble of a short jacket with a flowing floor-length skirt. Her long thick hair was neatly tied back. With an air of enigmatic desolation masking her countenance, her allure was distinctly incongruous with her position as an errand girl in a place like this.

'Well . . . Mr Kim?'

'Hello. I'm so glad to see you. I've brought someone here who might appreciate your hobby.'

Once again Ji-uk was mystified by the secret codes in their exchanges.

'How about it? If it's all right with you, shall I introduce you to this girl's peculiar habit?' Kim became talkative again. He was still not quite satisfied with a simple introduction. By posing this question to Ji-uk he was about to meddle in Ji-uk's affairs. Even before Ji-uk had a chance to answer they began drinking the wine served by the woman. He followed up what he had begun to ask, while handing his wine cup to Ji-uk across the table after drinking from it first.

'This girl has a habit of combing her hair whenever she has a free moment. How she developed this habit is something of a mystery.' He seemed to have planned all this in advance.

'You're making a joke out of it again, Mr Kim,' the girl protested, trying to discourage Kim from saying more.

'Please don't interrupt. There is nothing to feel shy about.'

Kim went on with his story. When a certain traveller had entered the inn one day, the girl had been sitting by the corner of the *maru* combing her hair. The people in the inn thought him to be a man of eccentric tastes, judging from the way he insisted on having her serve him his wine. After the drink, they spent the night together. It was assumed that something had taken place between them that night because afterwards she developed the habit of combing her hair. This was why she was known as the 'Hair Princess' and why she had gained a reputation as a lazy girl who thought of nothing but combing her hair.

'I still don't have any idea what happened between them that night. This princess's lips are sealed. Am I right?' Kim asked, prodding her one more time in the hope of coaxing a reaction from her.

The young woman sat calmly, filling the cups as soon as the guests had drained them, a gentle smile hovering on her lips. She showed no inclination to protest, or possibly she was unable to deny Kim's account.

'Then how about this?' Kim proposed to Ji-uk half in jest. 'Why don't you try to find out about it tonight?' But his proposition sounded in earnest, for Kim's expression suggested that there was a definitive conclusion to be reached. There must surely be a reason for this, Ji-uk thought, remembering that Kim had asked for this particular girl to serve them. Unable to read Kim's intention, however, Ji-uk hesitated to respond to his question.

She might be the songstress, the thought flashed through his mind. But it was obvious that she could not be, for she was too young; moreover, she was not blind. Still, it took some time for him to erase the impression from his mind.

'Well, I doubt that she would tell me anything that you don't already know. Is she by any chance a pansori singer?' he asked simply for the sake of saying something.

At this precise moment, the question seemed to have caught Kim off-guard. 'This girl, you mean?' Kim asked, flustered, and then denied it vehemently. 'No, she is no singer, I am quite sure. But then, if you are curious about it, you could find that out for yourself from her tonight.'

But in Kim's exaggerated tone of voice, Ji-uk read a less

clear meaning in his suggestion. It could be interpreted as the opposite of what Kim had just said, find it out himself tonight. Ji-uk found it strange that Kim did not insist on getting a response from him and remained silent, seemingly satisfied with what he had accomplished.

'Excuse me for a moment,' Kim said finally, standing up. Ji-uk thought he needed to go to the toilet, observing his abrupt movement. Then, just before disappearing through the door, Kim stopped and added, 'I almost forgot to tell you about the man, the traveller who produced such a lasting impression on her. You might know who he is if she tells you about him. He was none other than the man I told you about, the man who had searched so long for his pansori-singing half-sister. I hope this will help you to sort things out.'

Kim left the room in a hurry. Those words would turn out to be his parting words. Ji-uk waited, but there was no sign of him returning. He felt awkward drinking alone with the girl and tried to find out from her the reason for Kim's sudden departure. 'Mr Kim must surely be gone. The last train is about to leave now,' she told him.

'He usually leaves in this manner. If you don't believe me, you can ask the cashier.' She added that she had not paid any particular attention to his disappearance because she was used to his ways.

It was the strangest way of parting. Ji-uk was incredulous. So on his way to use the washroom he went to the cashier to verify what he had heard. It was just as the girl had said. Kim had paid for everything and left. Dazed, he stood in the dark, but realizing that it would be hopeless to wait for Kim to return he went back to the room.

The girl was waiting for Ji-uk, but the sight of her startled him. The wine table had been pushed into the corner. Grasping a large comb with one hand and holding her long lustrous hair with the other, she combed single-mindedly and vigorously.

In this vision before him Ji-uk saw the image of a living word. He had no other choice that night but to bear the weight of its meaning.

NOTES

1 *The Song of Chunhyang*, the tale of a faithful wife (see pages 13–15 for a more detailed description of this pansori).

2 From *The Song of the Water Palace*, a cautionary tale of foolishness (see pages 16–17 for a more detailed description of this pansori).

3 *Sarang* quarters are separate quarters for the man of the house where he receives and entertains his guests.

4 Based on *The Song of Hongbo and Nolbu* (see pages 17–18 for a more detailed description of this pansori), a traditional tale of brotherly love.

5 Based on the legend of Sim Cheong, a tale of a daughter's filial piety.

6 The floor plan of a modest traditional Korean house is L-shaped, and the essential components are a kitchen, a *maru* – a hardwood-floored room – and a bedroom. The living quarters are elevated, and a stepping stone provides entry to the *maru*, which serves as the place in which the family takes informal meals, when weather permits, and receives guests.

7 Before a pansori performance the singer usually warms up and establishes the musical mood by performing a *tan-ga* or short epic song which requires the same kind of vocal techniques as pansori and contains similar melodic themes but is easier to sing because of its non-dramatic nature.

8 The extant pansori repertoire is limited to a few songs, the most common among them being *The Song of Chunhyang*, *The Song of Sim Cheong* (see pages 15–16 for a more detailed description of

this pansori) and *The Song of Hongbo and Nolbu*. Singers learn by closely following the styles of master singers.

9 A health drink.

10 Letters from the Korean alphabet, hangeul.

11 A primer for learning Chinese characters.

12 Before the invention of the Korean alphabet, hangeul, in 1446 Koreans wrote in Chinese; however, most scholarly writings and official documents continued to be written in Chinese until the early twentieth century.

13 Seon is a Buddhist sect known better in the West as Chan Buddhism (China) or Zen Buddhism (Japan).

14 So-chi was the pen name of Heo Ryeon (1809–1892), who was renowned for his poetry, paintings and calligraphy.

Also published by Peter Owen

THE REVERSE SIDE OF LIFE
Lee Seung-U

978-0-7206-1259-2 • PB • 208pp • £10.95

'One of the best contemporary Korean authors' – *Valeurs Actuelles*

'Few contemporary Korean writers match Lee in his treatment of solemn subjects . . . He is unequalled in conveying the idea of original sin that lies beneath all human actions and of a God who stands by like an adult observing a child at play.' – *Korea Times*

Bak Bugil's father was a genius, but he disappeared after going to study in Seoul. Bak lives with his mother and his father's relatives. At the back of the house is a persimmon tree and a ramshackle hut. Children are forbidden to go near the tree, but Bak makes repeated incursions to collect its fruit until a chance encounter with the hut's inhabitant changes his life for ever . . . Years later a journalist is asked write about Bak, now one of South Korea's most original writers, and decides to reconstruct the author's childhood through an examination of his works. When he meets Bak it becomes clear that the author finds such recollections traumatic. Underpinning his earliest memories is a face lonely and dark. The journalist knows that to penetrate Bak's psyche he must first confront that face.

In this semi-autobiographical novel, a hit in German and French, Lee Seung-U (b. 1959) explores his own roots and the concept of a distant God who only occasionally extends a helping hand, to reveal how the conflict of the secular and the divine manifests itself in the real world. This extraordinary novel cemented its author's reputation as a star of South Korea's literary scene.

Peter Owen books can be purchased from:
Central Books, 99 Wallis Road, London E9 5LN, UK
Tel: +44 (0) 845 458 9911 Fax: + 44 (0) 845 458 9912
e-mail: orders@centralbooks.com

www.peterowen.com

NATSUME SOSEKI (1867–1916) is Japan's most revered writer and one of the great writers of the twentieth century – described by the *Sunday Telegraph* as the 'greatest Japanese novelist of the modern period' – whose works continue to attract critical scrutiny and debate. Educated at Tokyo Imperial University, he was sent to England in 1900 as a government scholar. As one of the first Japanese writers to be influenced by Western culture, he is read by virtually all Japanese, and his influence, both on contemporary Japanese authors and throughout East Asia and beyond, has been immense.

The Tower of London

Soseki's acutely observed recollections of his experience as a Japanese scholar in Victorian London. He develops profound reflections on universal themes: the Thames is transformed into the Styx; the Tower of London becomes a gateway to the Underworld; spirits of the dead are encountered through relics and memoir.

PB / 978-0-7206-1234-9 / £14.99

'One is never in doubt that one is in the presence of greatness' – *Spectator*

The Gate

The Gate describes the everyday world of humble clerk Sosuke and his wife Oyone, a childless couple, whose quiet world is rocked first by the appearance of Sosuke's brother then the news that Oyone's estranged ex-husband will be visiting near by. Understated, poetic and profound.

PB / 978-0-7206-1250-9 / £9.95

'A sensitive, skilfully written novel' – *Guardian*

Kokoro

A meditation on the changing Japanese culture and its attitudes to honour, friendship, love and death, *Kokoro* is also a sly subversion of all these things. The novel describes the friendship between the narrator and the man he calls 'Sensei', who is haunted by mysterious events in his past until the truth is revealed in tragic circumstances.

PB / 978-0-7206-1297-4 / £9.95

'A brilliant piece of narrative' – *Spectator*

The Three-Cornered World

A painter escapes to a mountain spa to work in a world free from emotional entanglement but finds himself fascinated by the enigmatic mistress at his inn, and, inspired by thoughts of Millais' *Ophelia*, he imagines painting her. Somehow the right expression for the face eludes the artist . . .

PB / 978-0-7206-1357-5 / £9.99

'A writer to be judged by the highest standards' – *Spectator*

Also published by Peter Owen

SHUSAKU ENDO is widely regarded as one of the greatest Japanese authors of the late twentieth century. Born in 1923, he won many major literary awards and was nominated for the Nobel Prize. As a Catholic Japanese (at a time when the Christian population of Japan was less than 1 per cent) and suffering from chronic ill health, he wrote from the perspective of the outsider. His novels, which have been translated into twenty-eight languages, include *The Sea and Poison*, *Wonderful Fool*, *Deep River*, *The Samurai*, *Scandal* and *Silence*. He died in 1996.

Silence

Endo's masterpiece, a haunting tale of tested faith, apostasy and martyrdom in feudal Japan, *Silence* follows Portuguese missionaries as they secretly travel the country to minister to the persecuted Catholic Japanese. To be filmed by Martin Scorsese.
Peter Owen Modern Classic / 978-0-7206-1286-8 / £10.95
'One of the finest historical novels written by anyone, anywhere . . . Flawless' – David Mitchell

The Samurai

In 1613 four Samurai set sail to bargain for a Catholic crusade through Japan in exchange for trading rights with the West. On their return they find that the Shoguns have turned against the West and are persecuting Christians. Disgraced and tormented, the Samurai begin to identify with the crucified Christ they formerly reviled.
Peter Owen Modern Classic / 978-0-7206-1185-4 / £10.95
'Genius . . . makes the imagination take wing' – *Mail On Sunday*

Scandal

An eminent Japanese-Catholic novelist is about to receive a major literary award. When a drunk woman he has never met claims she knows him well from his visits to Tokyo's red-light district, surely she must be mistaken? A dark, metaphysical and psychological thriller.
Peter Owen Modern Classic / 978-0-7206-1241-7 / £9.95
'Endo's most remarkable novel . . . a superb dramatic triumph'
– *Independent*

Also available ISBN prefix 978-0-7206
Deep River 0920-2/HB/£15.95 • *The Final Martyrs* 0870-0/HB/£14.99
The Girl I Left Behind 0932-5/HB/£14.99 • *The Golden Country* 0758-1/HB/£14.50
Stained Glass Elegies 0629-4/HB/£14.95 • *Volcano* 0510-5/HB/£14.50
Wonderful Fool 1320-9/POMC/£9.99

Peter Owen books can be purchased from:
Central Books, 99 Wallis Road, London E9 5LN, UK
Tel: +44 (0) 845 458 9911 Fax: + 44 (0) 845 458 9912
e-mail: orders@centralbooks.com

www.peterowen.com

The Seven Churches
MILOŠ URBAN (*translated by Robert Russell*)
The Seven Churches is a bloody, atmospheric modern Gothic classic, a bestseller in Czech, Spanish and German. Set in Prague's medieval quarter, the narrator witnesses a series of mysterious murders, triggering unsettling meetings with Gothic characters who appear to be trying to reconstruct medieval Prague within the modern city.
PB / 978-0-7206-1311-7 / £8.99
'The Czech Republic's answer to Umberto Eco' – *Radio Prague*

Birdbrain
JOHANNA SINISALO (*translated by David Hackston*)
Birdbrain is a skilful portrait of the unquenchable desire of Westerners for the pure and the primitive. A Finnish couple go on a hiking trip in Australasia with only *Heart of Darkness* as reading material. But what happens when nature starts to fight back?
PB / 978-0-7206-1343-8 / £9.99
'A sense of horror that will leave you troubled for weeks' – *Guardian*

Not Before Sundown
JOHANNA SINISALO (*translated by Herbert Lomas*)
In this award-winning bestseller, a gay photographer finds a young troll and takes him home. It seems, however, that trolls exude pheromones that have a profound aphrodisiac effect on all those around them, and the troll becomes the interpreter of man's darkest, most forbidden impulses.
PB / 978-0-7206-1350-6 / £9.99
'A punk version of *The Hobbit*' – *USA Today*

The Same River
JAAN KAPLINSKI (*translated by Susan Wilson*)
The Same River is the first novel by celebrated poet and essayist Jaan Kaplinski. Semi-autobiographical, it describes a young man's life, dominated by oriental studies, poetry and love, in Tartu, Soviet Estonia, in the 1960s. But when he finds himself under investigation for his relationship with an older poet, his life is changed for ever.
PB / 978-0-7206-1340-7 / £9.99
'A new light in the European galaxy' – *Independent*

Peter Owen books can be purchased from:
Central Books, 99 Wallis Road, London E9 5LN, UK
Tel: +44 (0) 845 458 9911 Fax: + 44 (0) 845 458 9912
e-mail: orders@centralbooks.com

www.peterowen.com

SOME AUTHORS WE HAVE PUBLISHED

James Agee • Bella Akhmadulina • Tariq Ali • Kenneth Allsop
Alfred Andersch • Guillaume Apollinaire • Machado de Assis • Miguel Angel Asturias
Duke of Bedford • Oliver Bernard • Thomas Blackburn • Jane Bowles • Paul Bowles
Richard Bradford • Ilse, Countess von Bredow • Lenny Bruce • Finn Carling
Blaise Cendrars • Marc Chagall • Giorgio de Chirico •Uno Chiyo • Hugo Claus
Jean Cocteau • Albert Cohen • Colette • Ithell Colquhoun • Richard Corson
Benedetto Croce • Margaret Crosland • e.e. cummings • Stig Dalager • Salvador Dali
Osamu Dazai • Anita Desai • Charles Dickens • Fabián Dobles • William Donaldson
Autran Dourado • Yuri Druzhnikov • Lawrence Durrell • Isabelle Eberhardt
Sergei Eisenstein • Shusaku Endo • Erté • Knut Faldbakken • Ida Fink
Wolfgang George Fischer • Nicholas Freeling • Philip Freund • Carlo Emilio Gadda
Rhea Galanaki • Salvador Garmendia • Michel Gauquelin • André Gide
Natalia Ginzburg • Jean Giono • Geoffrey Gorer • William Goyen • Julien Gracq
Sue Grafton • Robert Graves • Angela Green • Julien Green • George Grosz
Barbara Hardy • H.D. • Rayner Heppenstall • David Herbert • Gustaw Herling
Hermann Hesse • Shere Hite • Stewart Home • Abdullah Hussein
King Hussein of Jordan • Ruth Inglis • Grace Ingoldby • Yasushi Inoue
Hans Henny Jahnn • Karl Jaspers • Takeshi Kaiko • Jaan Kaplinski • Anna Kavan
Yasunuri Kawabata • Nikos Kazantzakis • Orhan Kemal • Christer Kihlman
James Kirkup • Paul Klee • James Laughlin • Patricia Laurent • Violette Leduc
Lee Seung-U • Vernon Lee • József Lengyel • Robert Liddell • Francisco García Lorca
Moura Lympany • Dacia Maraini • Marcel Marceau • André Maurois • Henri Michaux
Henry Miller • Miranda Miller • Marga Minco • Yukio Mishima • Quim Monzó
Margaret Morris • Angus Wolfe Murray • Atle Næss • Gérard de Nerval • Anaïs Nin
Yoko Ono • Uri Orlev • Wendy Owen • Arto Paasilinna • Marco Pallis • Oscar Parland
Boris Pasternak • Cesare Pavese • Milorad Pavic • Octavio Paz • Mervyn Peake
Carlos Pedretti • Dame Margery Perham • Graciliano Ramos • Jeremy Reed
Rodrigo Rey Rosa • Joseph Roth • Ken Russell • Marquis de Sade • Cora Sandel
George Santayana • May Sarton • Jean-Paul Sartre • Ferdinand de Saussure
Gerald Scarfe • Albert Schweitzer • George Bernard Shaw • Isaac Bashevis Singer
Patwant Singh • Edith Sitwell • Suzanne St Albans • Stevie Smith
C.P. Snow • Bengt Söderbergh • Vladimir Soloukhin • Natsume Soseki
Muriel Spark Gertrude Stein • Bram Stoker • August Strindberg
Rabindranath Tagore • Tambimuttu • Elisabeth Russell Taylor • Anne Tibble
Roland Topor • Miloš Urban • Anne Valery • Peter Vansittart • José J. Veiga
Tarjei Vesaas • Noel Virtue • Max Weber • Edith Wharton • William Carlos Williams
Phyllis Willmott • G. Peter Winnington • Monique Wittig • A.B. Yehoshua •
Marguerite Young • Fakhar Zaman • Alexander Zinoviev • Emile Zola